JOE COLTON

I've always loved my niece, Liza, like a daughter.
A beautiful and talented singer, Liza was groomed
from childhood by my pushy sister-in-law to be a
star. Now, I never understood why my younger
brother, Graham, married an ice princess like
Cynthia in the first place.... Over the years, Liza
has bent over backward to win her mother's
love—yet to no avail. Still, Liza has always known
that she has a safe haven with Meredith and me in
Prosperino whenever she needs it. Unfortunately,
it looks like the strain of the disappearance of
her beloved foster cousin Emily, and her stressful
nationwide tour have finally taken their toll on
her. Funny how Liza seems much less distraught
about losing her voice than her mother is. One
might even say Liza's relieved to be out of the
spotlight. Hmm...maybe her new outlook on life
has something to do with that compassionate
specialist, Dr. Nick Hathaway, who has taken on
her case. From what I hear, the dashing doc is
working miracles on my niece's aching heart!

About the Author

JUDY CHRISTENBERRY

has never been enthralled with a doctor until
Dr. Nick Hathaway became a part of her world. But
she's perfectly content for him to fall for Liza Colton.
After all, the beautiful singer resembles Audrey Hepburn,
Judy's favorite actress. So, writing their story for the
incredible series THE COLTONS has been a particular
pleasure. Their sprawling family has variety for everyone.
This bestselling author, who's been selling her stories for
twelve years, always loves the happy endings for both
her and her characters. She hopes you do, too.

Judy Christenberry

The Doctor Delivers

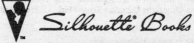

Published by Silhouette Books

America's Publisher of Contemporary Romance

Special thanks and acknowledgment are given
to Judy Christenberry for her contribution
to THE COLTONS series.

SILHOUETTE BOOKS
300 East 42nd St.,
New York, N. Y. 10017

ISBN 0-373-38707-5

THE DOCTOR DELIVERS

Visit Silhouette at www.eHarlequin.com

Printed in U.S.A.

THE COLTONS

Meet the Coltons—
a California dynasty with a legacy of privilege and power.

Liza Colton: *The dynasty's diva.* During a national tour that could fulfill her parents' ambitions, this up-and-coming starlet suddenly has a change of heart. Could it have something to do with her handsome doctor's bedside manner?

Nick Hathaway: *A family man.* His marriage to a self-absorbed blue blood had been a bitter pill for this doctor to swallow. And though he was strongly attracted to his celebrity patient, he had no doubt that she was cut from the same piece of silk. Even if her warmhearted actions seemed to prove just the opposite!

Meredith "Patsy" Colton: *A dangerous bedfellow.* Frustrated at her attempts to find her sibling and to kill that "bothersome" Emily Blair, Joe Colton's impostor wife has just stepped up her campaign....

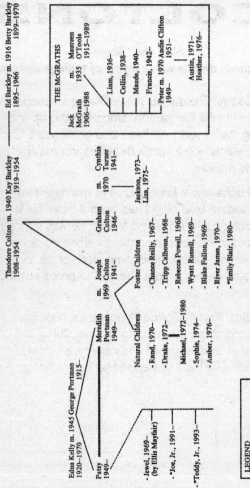

THE COLTONS

Theodore Colton m. 1940 Kay Barkley ——— Ed Barkley m. 1916 Betty Barkley
1908–1954   1919–1954   1895–1966   1899–1970

THE McGRATHS

Jack   m.   Maureen
McGrath   1935   O'Toole
1906–1988   1915–1989

- Liam, 1936–
- Collin, 1938–
- Maude, 1940–
- Francis, 1942–
- Peter m. 1970 Andie Clifton
  1949–   1951–
  - Austin, 1971–
  - Heather, 1976–

Edna Kelly m. 1945 George Portman
1920–1970   1915–

Meredith
Portman
1949–

m. 1969

Joseph   Graham   Cynthia
Colton   Colton   Turner
1941–   1946–   1941–

m. 1970

- Jackson, 1973–
- Liza, 1975–

Foster Children
- Chance Reilly, 1967–
- Tripp Calhoun, 1968–
- Rebecca Powell, 1968–
- Wyatt Russell, 1969–
- Blake Fallon, 1969–
- River James, 1970–
- *Emily Blair, 1980–

Natural Children
- Rand, 1970–
- Drake, 1972–
- Michael, 1972–1980
- Sophie, 1974–
- Amber, 1976–

Patty
1949–

- Jewel, 1969–
  (by Ellis Mayfair)
- *Joe, Jr., 1991–
- Teddy, Jr., 1993–

LEGEND
- - - Child of Affair
| Twins
* Adopted by Joe Colton

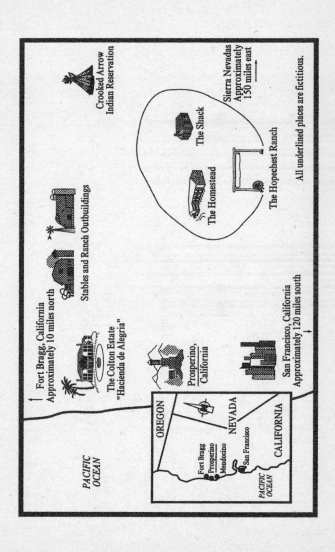

Crooked Arrow
Indian Reservation

The Shack

Sierra Nevadas
Approximately
150 miles east →

The Homestead

The Hopechest Ranch

All underlined places are fictitious.

Stables and Ranch Outbuildings

Fort Bragg, California
Approximately 10 miles north

The Colton Estate
"Hacienda de Alegria"

Prosperino,
California

San Francisco, California
Approximately 120 miles south

PACIFIC
OCEAN

OREGON

NEVADA

CALIFORNIA

Fort Bragg
Prosperino
Mendocino
San Francisco

PACIFIC
OCEAN

One

"**D**octor, you'll never guess who's here to see you!"

Liza Colton's head snapped up. Her glance around the room confirmed that she was still alone in the examination room, waiting for the busy doctor's attention. Her gaze focused on the door, realizing it wasn't quite closed.

"Missy, I don't have time for guessing games." The deep voice had an interesting, intriguing timbre that fascinated Liza. She wondered if his appearance could possibly match his voice. Not that it mattered, really.

"But it's the latest diva!" the invisible nurse gushed.

Liza stiffened.

"Diva?"

As if the nurse thought he didn't understand the word, she said, "You know, that's what they call Streisand, Céline Dion, Mariah Carey—"

"I know what the word means, Missy," the male voice asserted. "I'm just surprised, though. What diva would be here in Saratoga Springs?" But there wasn't an ounce of interest in his voice.

"Liza Colton! I saw her two nights ago. She's the latest diva. Well, she will be. She's not quite there yet. But she was fabulous! Why, she got a standing ovation at the end. Everyone just kept on clapping."

Liza smiled. It had been a gratifying moment. And she hadn't had too many of those lately.

"The beer sales must've been brisk," he said dryly. "Why is she here?"

"It's tragic! She can barely speak."

"After performing two nights ago?"

"And last night, too. And she's got another performance tonight." There was a brief pause, and Liza thought maybe they'd moved away. Which suited her just fine. The man obviously didn't appreciate music or have much regard for her talents.

"Oh, Doctor," the nurse, who'd shown her into the examining room, pleaded, her overwrought tones making Liza roll her eyes, "you just have to save her!"

"Let's don't get carried away, Missy. I'm an ear, nose and throat specialist, not a heart surgeon."

Well, unlike most doctors, at least he didn't have an inflated view of himself. Liza decided maybe she could forgive him for his earlier remarks.

Then the door opened.

She was skilled at cloaking her emotions—good thing—but she'd never been bowled over by a man's looks before.

He was gorgeous. Not picture perfect, like the models or actors who tried to impress her. She wasn't sure how she knew, but he had…substance. That was the word she was searching for. Gorgeous substance. His dark brown hair was conservatively cut, but rumpled, as if he ran his hands through it…and made her want to do the same. His physique was that of an athlete, strong, muscular. And his blue eyes almost made her swoon. Or was that her illness?

"Ms. Colton?" he asked as he stepped into the room and extended his hand.

She was reluctant to accept that offer of welcome. But she finally shook his warm hand with hers. And shivered.

"Cold? Oh, sorry, I forgot to introduce myself. I'm Dr. Hathaway."

She gave him a slight smile and nodded.

"I understand you've been exciting the crowds with your singing. Congratulations."

She wanted to ask if he paid his nurse a bonus for filling him in on his patients so he could appear so interested. But he wasn't worth straining her voice any further.

With a nod, she waited for him to get down to business.

"Can you tell me what the problem is?"

She drew a deep breath. Many men had told her

how sultry, how sexy, her voice was. But now it was raw, raspy and painful. With care, she said, "I've strained my voice."

When she said nothing else, he pulled out a tongue depressor. "Open up."

After several minutes of studying her throat and checking her ears, a frown on his well-chiseled face that, incredibly, included a cleft in his chin, he stepped back. "When did you first feel discomfort?"

"Last night," she whispered.

"After your performance?"

She nodded.

"Did it hit you suddenly?"

She shook her head no.

"Have you ever had this problem before?"

She shook her head. Then she said, carefully, "Stress. Antibiotics. Rest."

Nick Hathaway clamped down on the cynical laughter that rose in his throat. Typical of these spoiled, wealthy young women. She'd never had the problem before, but she'd already diagnosed it and determined the cure.

"And you came to see me so you could demonstrate your brilliant diagnostic skills?" He knew better than to use sarcasm on a patient, but she happened to be the kind of woman he avoided at all costs.

Beside being beautiful, she was wealthy and self-centered. He knew from experience how wealthy women worked. And with beauty added to the mix—

She spoke again in that painful voice. "Antibiotics."

He raised one eyebrow. "I don't dispense antibiotics on request, Ms. Colton." She just stared at him with the most glorious green eyes he'd ever seen. "I'll need to do a throat culture, run a few other tests."

She had the nerve to shake her head.

Nick glared at her, but she raised her left wrist and pointed to the watch she wore. A Rolex, of course.

"Theater," she whispered.

He couldn't believe her. "You surely don't think you're going to perform tonight?" Damn, the woman could barely speak.

She shrugged her shoulders.

"Look, Ms. Colton, if you are under my care, there will be no performance tonight. No performance for at least two weeks, at which time I will reevaluate your situation, but I promise nothing." He sounded too angry. Drawing a deep breath, he finished in cold tones, "If you find those terms unacceptable, I'll be glad to refer you to another local doctor. Or you can take yourself to New York City and a considerably more expensive doctor to confirm what I've just said."

Much to his surprise, after staring at him with various emotions changing those brilliant green eyes to a darker color, she gave a vigorous nod of approval. Then she whispered, "Antibiotics."

He was surprised at the relief that her agreement

gave him, but her last word irritated him again. "No antibiotics until after the tests."

Her eyes rounded in panic, and she vigorously shook her head no.

"Yes," he insisted. "I insist."

To his consternation, she slid off the examining table, picked up the purse she'd left in a side chair and started for the door.

He should let her go, he decided. He didn't need a patient unwilling to listen, intent on getting her way, determined to be in control.

Then she fainted.

Liza didn't come to until she'd been put in an ambulance. The clanging of the doors brought her around. There was a man beside the stretcher and she reached out to tug on his shirt.

"Just lie quietly, ma'am. We'll have you to the hospital in a couple of minutes."

She didn't need to be told the obvious. She tried again. "Doctor," she whispered, not seeing the handsome man who'd examined her.

"No, I'm not the doctor. I'm a paramedic." He grinned at her, no doubt impressed with his boyish charm.

She wasn't impressed by his intelligence. "Hathaway!" she returned, the strain sending shooting pains down her throat.

"Oh!" the young man exclaimed, as if a lightbulb had gone off over his head. "You mean where is Dr.

Hathaway?'' After she nodded, he added, ''He's meeting us at the hospital.''

Frowning, Liza thought about what had occurred. The doctor had wanted her to have tests. No doubt if she went to a hospital, he'd expect her to stay. She couldn't.

Grabbing his shirt again as the paramedic leaned forward to say something to his partner, who was driving the ambulance, she said, ''No hospital.''

''Hey, pretty lady, we've got a fine hospital. They'll take good care of you.''

She vigorously shook her head.

Ignoring her response, he said, his voice full of fake cheerfulness, ''Here we are.''

When they rolled her into the emergency room, she felt like the center of a whirlwind, not moving as everyone rushed around her.

The paramedic was giving a report to a doctor in abbreviated terms that made no sense to her. She tried to interrupt, but with no voice, it was hard to get their attention.

She used her earlier technique, grabbing the man's white coat and tugging.

''Hello, Ms. Colton. Don't worry. We're going to take care of you. I've heard you sing. Let me tell you it's a pleasure to welcome you to our hospital.''

She shook her head. ''No hospital,'' she insisted in her raspy whisper, her stress rising.

''Dr. Hathaway will be here any minute. I'm sure he—''

"No!" she protested as loudly as possible. Then she fell back against the pillow, clutching her throat.

For the first time the doctor appeared unsure of himself. "Uh, we'll just take your vital signs and wait for Dr. Hathaway." And he backed away from her, giving instructions to a nurse.

Liza closed her eyes. Being unable to use such a vital part of her, her voice, was frustrating. She knew she'd endangered it with her foolish behavior, but eating or sleeping had seemed unimportant the past three days.

If only she hadn't fainted.

"Ah, Dr. Hathaway, I'm glad you're here," she heard the E.R. doctor exclaim.

She shoved herself to a sitting position just as the nurse was trying to take her pulse.

"Here now, dear, just relax. Dr. Hathaway is one of our best physicians. He'll take good care of you."

She shook her head, her gaze seeking the handsome doctor. When she found him in the constantly moving crowd, she waved him over.

Before she could make the effort to speak, however, he began barking out orders to the nurse.

"And set up an IV. She's dehydrated." He looked at Liza. "When was the last time you ate?"

She shrugged her shoulders. She didn't want to admit her foolishness. But she'd been so frightened for Emily, it had been impossible to think of such mundane things.

While the nurse set up her IV, the E.R. physician drew Dr. Hathaway to the side and began whispering to him. He sent a sharp look her way, making Liza wonder what the man was telling him.

She had her answer when Dr. Hathaway stepped back to her side. "My cohort here says you've refused to be admitted."

She nodded, relieved that finally someone was listening to her.

"Look, Ms. Colton, I know you don't want to stay here, but at least let us give you some fluids and check things out. Only for an hour or two."

As he finished speaking, the nurse returned with a plastic bag of fluid.

"If you'll at least let us do that, you'll feel a lot better," he assured her, that deep voice sounding very soothing.

"Have to—call…cancel tonight," she muttered, each word paining her.

"Don't worry. I'll take care of it. What theater are you performing in?"

She managed to get out the name of the prestigious theater.

Even though he listened, he also motioned to the nurse. She placed something in his hand. He came around to the side of the bed where the IV was hung. "Just rest for a little while. I'll be back shortly," he assured her.

Liza saw him inject a syringe into a juncture in the tube. She tried to ask what he was giving her, but suddenly even her raspy whisper was impossible. Her tongue wouldn't move and her eyelids drifted closed.

The sleep that had eluded her for so long was making up for lost time.

"I want her admitted," Nick told his colleague.

"But she said she didn't want to be here," the E.R. doctor said cautiously. "We can't hold her against her will."

"Do you want to ask her now?"

"Well, no, I mean, you've sedated her, but—"

"She agreed to stay a few hours so we could check her out. I suspect she's either on some radical diet or may even have recently become bulimic. You know how these entertainers are." He turned to the nurse. "Have her taken upstairs and admitted. Tell the nurse on duty that at the first sign of her waking up, she's to call me at once."

"Yes, Doctor."

With a nod of thanks, he strode out of the emergency room to make the short drive back to his office. He'd left patients waiting while he attended to the mysterious Ms. Colton. The beautiful Ms. Colton.

Not that he was interested, of course, he assured himself. First of all, he never had personal relationships with his patients. And secondly, he'd been married to a beautiful, wealthy woman. He'd never commit such a mistake again.

Not that Liza Colton resembled his ex-wife, Daphne, in any way other than her wealth. Daphne was a neon sign and Liza Colton was moonlight. Daphne was a curvaceous blonde who used every trick in the book to catch a man's eye. Liza Colton was a slender brunette, almost too slender, her dark hair cut in a pixie that made her green eyes look huge. She had that fragile, graceful appearance of Winona Ryder or, maybe even more, Audrey Hepburn.

He shook off such thoughts. It wasn't like him to linger on a patient's appearance. His job was to treat the woman and send her on her way.

The rest of the afternoon he tended to patients, calmly and efficiently. But he couldn't keep his thoughts away from Liza Colton. He had his nurse call the hospital midway through the afternoon to check with the nurse on duty.

Ms. Colton was still sleeping.

He hadn't given her that strong a sedative. He'd expected her to awaken after a couple of hours.

As soon as he saw his last patient, he stripped off his lab coat and grabbed his jacket. "I'm going to the hospital, Missy. You can reach me there if anything comes up before you go home."

"Are you going to see Liza Colton? 'Cause I'd love her autograph!"

"She's sick, Missy. I can't bother her with that kind of request," he chided, smiling at his young nurse.

Missy's face fell. "I guess not."

Nick half smiled. "I'll see how she's feeling. Maybe I'll ask her, but I'm not promising anything." Missy was a good nurse who worked hard. Surely one autograph wouldn't be too much to ask from the diva.

He was rewarded by Missy's brilliant smile and her thanks. With a wave, he hurried to his car.

Once he reached the hospital, he went straight to the second floor where Liza Colton was. "Any change?" he asked the floor nurse.

"On Miss Colton? No, she's sleeping."

With a frown, he walked to her room. Just as the nurse had reported, she was sleeping soundly after four hours. Unless she had a bad reaction to the sedative, or she hadn't slept in a while, she shouldn't still be asleep.

He lifted her delicate hand and held her wrist. Pulse was normal. He listened to her heart. No problem there.

Reluctantly, he decided to awaken her.

"Ms. Colton? Can you hear me, Ms. Colton?" He patted her hand as he called her name, but she didn't stir. Finally he took her by her shoulders and gently shook her. "Liza? Liza, open your eyes."

Very slowly, her dark lashes swept up, and she stared at him blankly.

"Do you remember me? I'm Dr. Hathaway. You came to see me about your throat."

After staring at him with confusion, she finally nodded, then let her eyelids drift down again.

"Don't go back to sleep. I need to ask you some questions."

He grabbed the pillow from the next bed and pulled her forward, to slip the extra pillow behind her. He wasn't happy to realize he liked holding her in his arms. What was wrong with him suddenly?

He backed away from the bed and went to the foot of it, adjusting the upper part of it a little higher.

"Ms. Colton? Liza? Open your eyes."

"So tired," she whispered, even as her eyes flickered.

"Haven't you been sleeping well?"

"No," she said, her voice still raspy. "Couldn't."

"Why not?"

"Em—" Before she could finish that word, whatever it might've been, she came fully awake and sent a panicked look his way.

"What is it? What's wrong?" he asked, growing more intrigued by the moment. He went to the side of the bed.

"Have to go," she muttered, the words paining her if her face was any indication.

"You're not well, Ms. Colton. When's the last time you ate?"

With her gaze flickering around the room, as if looking for an escape, she shrugged her shoulders.

"Young lady, I need a better answer than that. If you're on some ridiculous, totally unnecessary diet, I need to know. It could be affecting your voice."

She lifted one thin hand to rub her forehead. "No," she replied, though he wasn't sure what she was saying.

"You're not on a diet?"

She shook her head, though not vigorously.

He leaned forward and pushed the call button. "Nurse? I want two dinner trays brought to room 226 ASAP."

"Yes, Doctor."

He sat on the edge of the bed. When she stared at

him in confusion, he said, "I'm starving. I thought I'd keep you company, even though it's a little early for dinner."

He wanted to see her eat. And keep the food down. If she was bulimic, he'd have to stay for several hours. But he hadn't really seen any signs of bulimia.

"Must go," she said, her raspy voice holding panic.

"I called the theater and told them you were ill and wouldn't be performing. They promised to take care of everything, and to keep your location quiet." He wasn't sure about that necessity, or even if that's what she'd want. She probably preferred the notoriety an illness would give her.

That was the way divas were.

The nurse came in at that moment carrying two trays.

"You're in luck tonight, Doctor. Meat loaf is on the menu, along with apple pie," the nurse told him, grinning.

He returned her smile. "Sounds good. Doesn't it, Ms. Colton?"

She looked so lost, he felt a stirring of compassion. If she was truly a diva, how had she lost her way so badly? Was someone pressuring her to lose weight? Was her career not going well? The theater said they'd contact her manager, and Nick had felt compelled to give them Liza's location to pass on to the man. But now he wondered if he'd made the right decision.

He moved to the foot of her bed to raise the head

of it a little more before he put one of the trays on the bed table and rolled it toward her. Then he removed the metal cover.

"Doesn't that look good?" he asked, looking at Liza.

She didn't move, her face not reflecting pleasure. Instead, she stared at the meal in distaste.

He ignored his own meal and lifted her fork to cut a piece of the thick meat loaf. "Let's take a bite of this. I think you'll really like it."

Holding it up to her mouth, he waited until she finally opened her lips for him to insert it.

He kept his eyes on her as he instructed, "Chew it up, Liza. You need the calories."

She swallowed and he started to feed her a bite of corn. Before he could, however, she emitted distressed sounds.

He grabbed the dish they distributed for queasy stomachs just in time.

Two

Embarrassed and miserable, Liza shuddered. "Too much."

"Lady, that was hardly enough to keep a fly alive," the doctor muttered, clearly irritated with her.

"No," she protested, her throat even more raw. "Haven't eaten since...days."

He stared at her as he checked her pulse. Then he punched the call button again. "Nurse, we need soup, Jell-O, things for nausea."

"I asked you when you last ate," he grumbled as he sat back after disposing of the pan. Then his eyes gentled. "Want me to wipe your face?"

She nodded, not bothering to speak. He disappeared, then reappeared, a damp washcloth in his hand. His gentleness as he cleaned her brought tears to her eyes.

"Hey, quit worrying. We're going to take care of you," he assured her.

"Have to go," she whispered.

"Honey, I don't think you have enough energy to walk. Why don't you tell me what's going on? I'll be better able to help you if you do."

She couldn't tell him about Emily. It was supposed to be kept secret. Especially what she knew.

The phone rang, startling her.

After raising one eyebrow at her, Nick Hathaway reached for the phone. Whoever it was could talk to him. He didn't want his patient straining her voice any more.

"Who's this?" a woman barked into the phone.

"Dr. Hathaway. Who's this?"

"Cynthia Turner Colton. Liza's mother and manager. Where's my daughter?"

"Your daughter is here in bed, Mrs. Colton, resting. May I help you?"

"No! Put her on the phone!"

"I'm sorry, Mrs. Colton, but I don't want your daughter to talk right now. Her throat has been damaged enough."

"Damaged?" the woman shrieked. "Damn it! You're a doctor. Fix it!"

"I'm doing what I can."

"I want her on that stage tonight, do you hear me? I will not allow her to screw up her reputation by missing concerts. People will start to whisper about drugs.''

''She can't—''

''Give her whatever is necessary for her to sing! Tell her I said she has no choice!''

''You're wrong. She's an adult.'' Even as he said those words, he stared at his patient. He'd assumed she was. He couldn't remember her age on the chart and she certainly looked young. When the woman on the phone didn't contradict him, he continued, ''She will choose whether or not she sings or remains my patient.''

''You uncooperative— I'll find another doctor. Get out of her room!''

Big green eyes were fixed on his face and he smiled, hoping to reassure her. ''As I said, Mrs. Colton, that's not your decision.''

''I'm her manager, damn you! Her career is my business. No two-bit country doctor is going to tell me what to do!''

Nick did something he'd never done before. He hung up on a family member of a patient. Because of her, he had a lot more sympathy for Liza Colton. Her mother/manager had never asked how Liza felt, if she was being well taken care of, or even if she was breathing. All she wanted was for her daughter to perform, whether she could or not.

''Your mother,'' he said, looking at Liza.

''Sorry,'' Liza whispered.

The nurse brought in a new tray and picked up the

old one. Nick had slid it away from the bed when she'd gotten sick. "Thanks, Mary."

She left and he smiled down at Liza. "Let's try this again with something a little easier on your system." He lifted a spoon to dip into the chicken broth when the phone rang again.

He had no doubt who was calling. Picking up the phone he said, "Yes?"

"Don't you hang up on me or I'm going to report you."

"Feel free. Want a number to call?"

"I want to talk to my daughter!"

"I'm sorry, that's not possible tonight. You can try again tomorrow. She might be available then."

"Tomorrow is too late! I want her on that stage tonight!"

"Mrs. Colton, I've already canceled her performance tonight. Any attempt to perform could do irreparable damage to her vocal cords. Is that what you want?"

"How qualified are you?"

"I'm an ear, nose and throat specialist with advanced degrees. I've been practicing in Saratoga Springs for eight years. I'm on the board here at the hospital and I consult around the state."

"So you'll guarantee she'll only miss tonight?"

"I'll do no such thing. She'll have to rest for two weeks. Then we'll see." He knew his words were going to set her off again, so he held the receiver away from his ear. Liza had closed her eyes, but as her mother's voice echoed from the receiver, she looked up at him, a sad expression on her face.

"I have to go now, Mrs. Colton. Thank you for calling." He didn't wait for her to respond, but he decided she couldn't really say he'd hung up on her again since he'd politely said goodbye. At least her call had shed a little more light on her daughter's emotional state, if nothing else.

He lifted the spoon half-filled with chicken broth to her lips and she slowly sipped. Then she tried to speak. "I can—" She reached for the spoon.

Though he allowed her to feed herself, he sat beside her until she'd eaten at least half the broth. "Want some of this tasty red Jell-O?" he asked, nudging the other bowl forward.

She frowned at the Jell-O, as if suspicious of it, but she finally slipped a trembly cube of it into her mouth. Lying back, she seemed to let it melt.

"Has your mother been pushing you to lose weight?" He couldn't imagine why the woman would want that. He thought Liza was too thin, but stage mothers could be crazy.

She shook her head and closed her eyes, as if hiding something.

"You know you've been playing a dangerous game not only with your health, but also your voice. The vocal cords are dependent on your overall health."

She nodded, but looked away.

"Try to eat a little more." When she picked up the spoon again, relief filled him. He was always concerned with his patients' recovery, but Liza Colton had grabbed his heart. Maybe it was the abusive mother. Or the sadness in her eyes. Or her overall fragility.

Several minutes later, she put down the spoon. "No more," she muttered, adding a small smile, as if to reward him.

"You did pretty well, considering that was your first meal in a while."

Liza could feel herself coming to depend on that sexy smile of the doctor's. And she was fascinated with the cleft in his chin. The urge to trace it with her finger was crazy, but it was there all the same.

She frowned, hoping to erase those thoughts and convince the doctor she was serious. "Must go."

Pushing the tray back, she tried to swing her legs off the bed, but he was blocking her way.

"I don't think so. Look, just give me twenty-four hours. We can—"

He broke off when she vigorously shook her head. And got dizzy.

"At least until the morning? I'll come to your room before you have breakfast. That will give you a night's rest, at least."

That plan sounded so tempting, she paused to give it some consideration. But Emily— "Call hotel," she whispered. "Messages."

She received a level stare for her words. "*I'll* call for your messages," he said. "They wouldn't understand you anyway."

She knew none of the family would leave any inappropriate messages for strangers to hear, so she nodded and gave him the name of the hotel. Tensely she waited for him to report back to her after his brief conversation.

"Your mother called half an hour ago, shortly before she reached you here. And a few minutes ago a Mrs. Tremble called."

Liza frowned. She wasn't surprised by her mother's calls. But Mrs. Tremble? Somehow that name rang a bell but— Suddenly she sat straight up in bed and grabbed the doctor's wrist.

"What is it? Are you in pain?" he asked at once, leaning close to her.

Too close. She drew a deep breath and subsided against the pillow. "Mrs. Tremble's message?"

He looked at the pad he'd written the messages on. "She said she'd call back in twenty-four hours."

Relief and joy filled Liza. "Number?"

He shook his head.

She had no way to return the call, but she reminded herself that Emily was smart. She been clever enough to elude the man who'd tried to kill her. Smart enough to be alive.

Liza wanted to call Uncle Joe, but she couldn't. Emily wouldn't have used the name Mrs. Tremble if everything was okay. Mrs. Tremble was an old rag doll that had been Emily's constant companion during her youth. She'd known Liza would recognize the name.

"What's so important about that call?" Dr. Hathaway asked.

She beamed at him. "Important," she repeated, nodding.

"So you'll stay overnight?" he asked, watching her.

What could it hurt? She could get a good night's rest and feel better tomorrow. And her mother probably wouldn't call back at the hospital. She wouldn't have to deal with her until she felt better.

That thought alone eased the tightness in her stomach. But most of all, it was Emily's call that had her relaxing, letting her exhaustion creep in, sending her eyelids lower. Emily was still in trouble, but she was alive.

Liza tried to nod, to signify her agreement, but she wasn't sure she made it. Blessed sleep was taking over.

Nick watched his patient fade into sleep, curiosity rampant in his head. When he'd read the message, her electric response told him it was important. Now, as he watched the tension leave her body, he knew whatever had been bothering her was easing, allowing sleep to take charge.

She should show a good improvement in the morning if she slept twelve or fourteen hours, after taking in some nourishment. He'd join her for breakfast, make sure she ate. Then, if she insisted on leaving he couldn't legitimately hold her.

But he thought he'd drop by the hotel and personally question the operator who had taken the message from the mysterious Mrs. Tremble.

Liza Colton had caught his interest for a lot of different reasons, not least of which was the mystery that surrounded her.

He insisted it had nothing to do with her delicate beauty.

It was Saturday, and the hospital was quiet at seven in the morning. Most doctors, if they made rounds, did so at a later hour on the weekends. But Nick didn't have family at home. Only his housekeeper. And he was used to the early hours.

At least that's how he justified his 7:00 a.m. arrival to himself. He was sure it had nothing to do with the fact that he'd dreamed about Liza Colton last night.

He'd stopped by the hotel on his way home and spoken to the woman who'd taken the messages for Liza. She'd told him that Mrs. Tremble had been a woman, sounding fairly young, and definitely not Mrs. Colton. The lady had rolled her eyes and remembering his own conversations with Liza's mother, Nick could understand that reaction.

That visit probably explained why he'd dreamed of his newest patient. It was the mystery. He read mysteries for relaxation. He loved the puzzle aspect, trying to figure out who the killer could be.

It couldn't be Mrs. Colton, he decided with a grin. She was much too obvious. But he suspected she had something to do with his patient's tension.

He stepped through the door of Liza's room, after having checked at the nurse's desk. Liza hadn't called for a nurse all night.

No wonder, he decided. She was still sleeping. She must've been on the verge of a total collapse when she'd come to his office. Quietly he moved to her side, sliding cool fingers down her arm to feel her pulse.

Her eyes slowly opened and she stared at him, no recognition in her eyes.

"Good morning, Liza. It's Dr. Hathaway. I seem to be in the habit of waking you up. How are you this morning?"

"F-fine," she managed, her voice low, husky, but not as raw as the night before.

"Good. I think breakfast is on the way. Do you want to use the facilities before you eat?"

She nodded. He pulled back the covers and helped her to stand. She swayed and his arm shot around her.

"I'll walk you to the door," he said, sounding as if his assistance was non-negotiable and normal. Slowly they crossed the small space. When they reached the door, he asked, "Can you make it on your own? I can call a nurse."

"Not necessary," she said softly and closed the door.

He stood outside the door, leaning one shoulder against the wall, anxious to have her back in the bed. He worried that she might fall and hurt herself even more.

The nurse came in carrying the two trays he'd requested.

"Morning, Doctor. How's the patient?"

"A little groggy."

The nurse looked at the closed door. "Want me to check on her?"

The door opened, making her offer unnecessary. Liza stood there, holding on to the doorjamb. "Robe?" she asked, looking at the nurse.

"'Fraid we don't have any. But don't worry. We've all seen backsides before," the nurse said cheerfully and put down the trays. "Call if you need me, Doctor." Then she swept out the door.

Liza stood there, her cheeks red. He figured she wasn't going to let him walk behind her to the bed, since her hospital gown tied in the back with revealing gaps. With a smile, he picked her up, holding her against his chest.

"This way, no one will see anything, including me," he promised her. The distance to the bed was ridiculously short, and he laid her down on the mattress.

"Ready for breakfast?" he asked, busying himself with putting the tray on the bed table and rolling it to her, then raising the head of the bed. Anything to dispel the memory of holding her against him.

He thought her eyes seemed brighter this morning. She gave the appearance of being stronger, even though she'd been trembling when she'd walked to the bathroom.

Lifting the metal covering from the plate, he revealed scrambled eggs, bacon, a biscuit and orange slices. "Hey, it looks good, doesn't it?"

She pointed to the second tray. "You eat, too."

"With pleasure. I didn't wake up my housekeeper this morning. I need coffee."

Her tray had milk instead of coffee, but she didn't complain.

He settled on the edge of the bed, a no-no as far as the nurses were concerned, but he wanted to be close to her. To observe her, of course. That was the only reason.

She needed no urging this morning to eat. But she filled up quickly. He noticed she hadn't eaten any bacon when she lay back against the pillows.

"Try a bite or two of bacon, in between orange slices," he suggested.

"I'm full."

"Just a bite or two. And the orange is especially sweet. You can't let it go to waste." He was pleased as he watched her do as he'd asked.

He'd almost finished his entire breakfast in the time it had taken her to eat half of hers. He stood and moved the bed tray as soon as she finished, stacking his empty tray beneath hers.

Then he returned to his seat on the bed and took her wrist in his hand. "So, how are you feeling now?"

"Much better, thank you," she whispered.

He took a tongue depressor and looked at her throat. Then he checked her ears. "You know what? I think your diagnosis was correct. You needed rest, food and no stress. And antibiotics." He grinned at her.

She smiled back. "Infection?"

"Maybe just the hint of one, but it's not unusual when the entire body is under this kind of pressure. We caught it early, so it will go away fast. Are you allergic to anything?"

She shook her head no.

"Then I'll be right back. Don't go away."

Liza watched the handsome doctor as he walked out of her room. He was being incredibly kind to her, especially after their confrontation in his office.

And because of him, she was feeling much better. Because of him and Emily's phone call. Liza was thinking more clearly this morning. She even thought she might have the strength to get downstairs and call a taxi. She certainly didn't want to cause the doctor any more trouble.

And she had to be back at the hotel for Emily's phone call. Emily Blair Colton was her cousin, but their closeness was greater than that and had a lot to do with Liza's own childhood.

Cynthia and Graham Colton, her mother and father, never showed any parental instincts. In fact, for as long as she could remember, Liza had considered her Aunt Meredith to be her true mother. She'd spent almost all summer every year at Uncle Joe and Aunt Meredith's home in California. Even most school holidays. Her mother was pleased to be rid of Liza and her brother. Even though they lived fairly close to Joe and Meredith, since her father worked for Joe, Cynthia and Graham never visited during her stays.

Always imaginative, Liza had built up a fantasy

that Meredith and Joe were her parents. Her time away from them was like boarding school. But she always came back to them.

From the moment Emily had been adopted by Meredith and Joe, Liza acted like her big sister, watching after her, making her feel more secure. Since she'd always longed for a sister, Liza took Emily to her heart. They'd become sisters by love if not by blood.

Nine years ago, while Liza was at her parents' house, her beloved Aunt Meredith had taken Emily in the car to see her biological grandmother. There'd been a wreck…and Aunt Meredith had never been the same.

Her interest in any of her children had disappeared at once. The garden she tended so enthusiastically was neglected. The strong bond she shared with her husband seemed to have disappeared, and Uncle Joe began staying away from home more than he ever had. And he seldom spent time with his wife, where before they'd been devoted to each other.

The next time Liza had come back to their home, she'd discovered Emily pale and frightened. Only to Liza did she tell her secret. She'd seen two Merediths the day of the accident: a good Meredith and bad Meredith.

Liza at first rejected Emily's story. But the longer she spent time around Aunt Meredith, the more she agreed that something horrible had happened. The woman she considered to be her mother seemed to have changed overnight. Both Emily and Liza had felt abandoned.

Though they'd kept in touch, she and Emily hadn't spent as much time together after the accident, because Cynthia launched Liza's singing career in earnest.

Then, a few days ago, Emily disappeared.

She'd called Liza the morning after her disappearance. Her tale of what had happened had scared Liza. Emily had promised to call again as soon as she could. Liza had been waiting for her call, afraid she might be trailed by the man Emily claimed had tried to do away with her earlier.

And she believed Emily's story. She believed Aunt Meredith had hired someone to kill Emily, in spite of the kidnapper's ransom note her uncle had received the next morning.

The door opened and she looked up, expecting either a nurse or Dr. Hathaway.

Instead, a strange man entered, dressed in jeans and a dirty blue shirt, a menacing look on his face and a long, sharp knife in his hand.

Three

Nick had gotten a prescription of antibiotics filled and was coming back to Liza's room when he noticed a man standing in the doorway.

"Excuse me," he said, smiling briefly. "Are you visiting Miss Colton?"

The man jerked in surprise and backed out of the door, tucking one hand behind his back, then turned and ran down the hall.

Nick's first concern was Liza. He stepped in the room to discover his patient pale and shaking. "Liza, what's wrong?"

"That—that man!" she exclaimed, her breathing shallow.

"You want me to stop him?"

She nodded urgently, but her eyes were fearful.

Nick shoved the medicine in his pocket, turned and ran for the elevators. At the nurse's desk, he said, "Call Security. Have them stop the man who just left this floor. He was wearing jeans and a blue shirt."

"He took the stairs," one nurse said even as she dialed the phone.

Nick did the same, racing down the stairs. He burst through the door into the main lobby, but despite a thorough search of the area, especially the front doors, he didn't see the man. Nick grabbed a security guard, but no one had seen the stranger.

"You want me to call the police, Dr. Hathaway?" the guard asked, eager to please.

"No, thanks, Pete. I'll talk to my patient. I think she's leaving the hospital today anyway."

"You just let us know, Doc. We'll do whatever you want."

"I know. I appreciate it, thanks." Nick took the elevator back to the second floor and returned to Liza's room.

"Who was that?" he asked as he entered.

"I—I don't know," she whispered, but she didn't look at him.

"I think you do. I want to know if the police should be involved."

He kept his gaze on her, but she didn't answer. Instead, she gnawed her bottom lip, fear in her eyes. He figured he had a right to intervene if for no other reason than her health. Whatever was bothering her had caused her not to eat or sleep.

It sounded pretty serious to him.

"Did he threaten you?"

She nodded her head.

"What did he say?"

" 'Where's Emily?' " she repeated, obviously quoting the man. Then she burst into tears.

Without even thinking about his actions, Nick strode across the room and pulled Liza against him, stroking her back in a soothing motion. When she began to calm down, he asked, "Did he say anything else?"

She shook her head.

"I hate to tell you this, but 'Where's Emily?' isn't much of a threat."

She sniffed and burrowed deeper against him. "He had a knife."

Nick asked enough to realize the knife was a serious weapon. "Okay, so who's Emily?"

At once, Liza stiffened and tried to draw away.

"Whoa, where do you think you're going?"

She avoided his gaze even as she put some distance between them. "I have to go."

"Where?"

"Back to the hotel."

"I'm not sure that's safe. What if the man finds you there?"

Her green eyes were huge as she thought about his words. "I—I don't think he'll come back," she whispered.

"Because you're going to call the police?"

She covered her face with her hands. "I don't

know what to do," she wailed, her words coming out muffled.

"You've got to stay calm, Liza, if you're going to get better. You have to concentrate on eating and sleeping. That's what's important."

She shook her head. "Emily is— I mean, other things— I have to go to the hotel."

Nick sat back and sighed. She might be weak. She might not have shown good judgment in skipping meals and sleep. But she was as stubborn as any woman he'd ever seen. "Okay, I'll take you to the hotel, if you'll let me come with you. And if you'll call the police."

"Maybe I should," she finally said with a sigh. Then she looked at him again, drilling him with her green eyes. "Do you promise to keep everything you overhear between me and the police a secret?"

"I promise," he said solemnly.

Once Dr. Hathaway got her to her room in the hotel, he told her to go shower and change clothes while he contacted the police.

"Ask for non-uniforms, please," she asked in a wobbly voice. "I don't want anyone in the hotel to wonder about the cops."

He nodded.

So far he'd done exactly as she'd asked in everything, so she decided to trust him. Besides, a shower and clean clothes were necessary before she could face anyone.

But she felt she had to report the man to the police

because she suspected he had something to do with Emily's disappearance. Uncle Joe had told her not to speak to anyone, but she thought he would agree to her telling the Saratoga Springs police. They could contact the police in Prosperino, California, where her uncle's huge estate was located.

Fifteen minutes later, she was exhausted but clean, dressed in black slacks and a green sweater, her hair still wet. She moussed and quickly styled it. Then she headed for the living room of her suite.

Dr. Hathaway stood as she entered and for the first time she noticed two other gentlemen in the room who also got to their feet. At least the police here were prompt.

"Liza Colton," the doctor said smoothly as he came forward and took her arm, "these gentlemen are John Ramsey and Bill Wilson, detectives with the Saratoga Springs Police Department."

He seemed to intuitively know she was feeling quite weak. Easing her into a nearby chair, he waved the officers back to the sofa. Then he hurried to answer a knock on her door.

Liza tensed, wondering if the knife-wielding stranger from the hospital had followed her back here. Instead, a waiter rolled in a cart. The doctor handed him some money and escorted him to the door.

"I ordered coffee," he told the detectives, "and a snack. Ms. Colton needs to eat. This is her first time on her feet and she's weak."

"I wouldn't mind a cup of coffee myself," one of

the detectives said before turning to her. "Can you tell me what the problem is, Ms. Colton?"

Liza licked her lips, fearful of what she had to say. She looked at Dr. Hathaway again, and he nodded in support. "My—my cousin was kidnapped several days ago. At least, that's what the ransom note said."

The men exchanged looks. "What is your cousin's name?" one of them asked.

"Emily Blair Colton." She noted the doctor's eyes narrowing, as he recognized the name. She added, "My uncle is Joe Colton. He's a former California senator." She knew his name would be much more recognizable than Emily's. He was a multi-millionaire, as well as politically active.

"And the man today? The doctor said he threatened you."

"Not exactly. He scared me by the way he stared at me, like he was going to hurt me, and he had a huge knife, but all he asked was where Emily was." Before the policemen could speak, she hurriedly added, "I know that's not a threat—" she spared the doctor a look "—but somehow I think he's connected to her kidnapping."

"You could be right. Can you describe him?"

"Yes."

"If I can borrow the phone, I'll call the station, see if we have any information on the kidnapping and request a police artist to come over."

At her nod, Detective Ramsey stood and crossed to the phone.

Dr. Hathaway put a glass of milk in front of her along with a plate of oatmeal raisin cookies.

"We'll help you eat those cookies," he said with a grin, "but you've got to have one or two, okay?"

"I just finished breakfast," she protested.

"That was several hours ago, and we both know you're a little behind in the nourishment department."

She blushed, aware of the other detective's sharp look. She certainly didn't want to explain anything else to these strangers. Including the fact that she'd talked to Emily after her escape and thought Emily was trying to contact her again.

She gasped and stared at the doctor. What if he mentioned the message from Mrs. Tremble?

He'd been watching her. "What?" he asked, kneeling beside her chair and reaching out to feel of her forehead. "Your throat hurt?"

"Uh, yes, a little."

He snapped his fingers. "I forgot to give you the antibiotics." He stood and pulled a pill bottle out of his pocket. "Here, take one of these morning and night until they're all gone."

Detective Ramsey returned to the sofa. "The police artist will be here in about fifteen minutes. Now, Ms. Colton, the kidnapping is being handled by the FBI. Our superintendent was quite surprised to discover anyone here knew about it."

She nodded.

With barely a pause, he continued, "Which made him wonder why someone involved in the kidnapping would come all this way to ask you about Ms. Colton.''

Liza had been lifting the milk glass to her mouth to help her swallow the pill, and his question caused the glass to wobble, splashing milk on the coffee table.

Dr. Hathaway quickly steadied her hand and helped her take a drink. It gave her time to think of her answer.

"Thank you," she said softly. She used a napkin to wipe up the spill. "I'm sorry, gentlemen. I'm a little weak today. To answer your question, Emily and I are very close, more like sisters than—than cousins. I suppose if—if she escaped from whoever took her, they would expect her to come to me."

"And you haven't seen her or talked to her?" Detective Wilson asked, both men's gazes fixed on her.

In spite of the temptation to look at the doctor, Liza faced her inquisitors and quietly said, "No. I've neither seen her nor talked to her. But I wish I had."

"Yes, ma'am," Ramsey said, nodding. "But do you have any idea where she might've gone if she escaped from whoever took her?"

"No," she said shaking her head. "But it's a good sign, isn't it? I mean, if the bad guys are looking for her, that means they don't have her, doesn't it?"

The two detectives exchanged a look. Then Ramsey said, "The ransom was paid yesterday, Ms. Colton. They didn't catch the guy who collected the money and your cousin hasn't been found."

"Maybe the man you saw today was her boy-friend," the second detective suggested.

"No! He was—he was in his forties and ugly." The doctor raised one of his eyebrows and she hastily said, "I don't mean ugly as in not handsome. I mean…not nice." She swallowed and rubbed her throat. Then she whispered, "Emily is only nineteen. She's so sweet, so gentle. She wouldn't have anything in common with this man."

The doctor got up to sit on the arm of her chair. "Lean back and breathe deeply, Liza. You're getting all tensed up again. And don't talk so much."

She did as he asked and closed her eyes. His close-ness helped her to take a deep breath. Strange how quickly she'd come to rely on him.

"We'll try to wrap this up quickly, Ms. Colton. We checked on the messages you've received here. One from your mother and another from a Mrs. Trem-ble. Can you tell me what they had to say?"

Nick felt the tension rise again in her. He quickly said, "If you don't mind me explaining, officers, to save my patient's throat, I spoke to her mother last night after she left the message here. Her mother is also her manager and she was concerned about Liza's schedule. There was no mention of Liza's cousin."

"And Mrs. Tremble?"

"I don't know who the woman is, but I can assure you Liza hasn't spoken to her. She spent the night in the hospital and received no calls. I've been with her since."

"Ms. Colton, if you could just—"

"Housekeeper," she said, her voice raspy again.

"And have you returned her call?" Ramsey asked.

She shook her head and pointed to her throat.

"Oh, that's right. Besides, she said she'd call today, didn't she?"

Liza nodded again but didn't try to speak.

"Is that all the questions, gentlemen?" Nick intervened. "I'd like her to save her voice to describe the man for the sketch artist."

"Yes, of course. What's wrong with Ms. Colton's throat?"

Nick looked at Liza, knowing he could refuse to say anything, but he feared to do so might make the men suspicious. And he had figured out that Liza was hiding something. "It's a combination of a slight infection and exhaustion. It seems she gave up eating or sleeping once she was told about her cousin's disappearance. She's been very concerned. It doesn't take the body long to deteriorate under those conditions."

A knock at the door signaled the arrival of the artist. Nick opened the door and invited him in. The two detectives, after greeting the man, picked up their cups of coffee and moved to the window to talk quietly.

Nick returned to the arm of Liza's chair. Her welcoming smile warmed his heart. She wanted him close. He reached for her glass of milk. "Take a drink before you try to speak again," he suggested.

She took the glass from him and took a long drink. Then she greeted the artist.

With gentle, perceptive questions, the artist drew Liza out as she described the man. Nick helped, since he'd also seen him. When the artist finished and held up the resulting sketch, both Nick and Liza agreed that he'd done a good job of drawing the man.

The two detectives came back to stand behind the sofa and look at the sketch.

"Do you recognize him?" Liza asked. When she looked at the sketch she gulped, her eyes wide with fear. The drawing was dead-on: a big, burly man with a full head of coal-black hair.

Nick reached for her hand and held it against his thigh. "Rest, Liza. Your throat is sounding worse again."

"No, ma'am, but he looks like a rough character, like an out-of-shape ex-fighter. He'd be pretty notice-able here in Saratoga Springs. We'll see if we can pick up a trace of him. I suspect he bribed one of the employees downstairs to give him your location. The doctor said he only told the hotel, with a warning not to let out the information, and the Music Hall people, with the same warning."

She nodded.

They sent the artist back to the station, with a request that he only show the sketch to the chief.

After he'd left, Ramsey sat back down on the sofa. "Now, Ms. Colton, what are your plans? Are you leaving the city?"

The lost look on her face bothered Nick. He wanted

to pull her into his arms and promise to keep her safe. A ridiculous thought! He had nothing to do with Liza Colton, popular singer. She probably had tons of people to keep her safe.

Like her mother? he wondered derisively. That woman wouldn't waste of moment of concern for her own daughter.

"I...don't know. Doctor—"

Nick took over. "My patient isn't well enough to travel yet. She'll stay in town for another day or two, I'm sure. But we'll let you know when she returns to New York City."

"You have a place there?" the detective asked.

She nodded. Then she added, "An apartment."

"Is that where Mrs. Tremble is?"

Nick felt her tense again. That name had set off her tension the last time.

"California," she whispered.

"Well, if you'll give us a number where you can be reached when you go back to New York City, we'll keep you updated on anything we find out," Ramsey said. Then he stood. "We'll go and let you rest." He started to walk to the door. Then he stopped and looked at Nick. "You going to stay with her? I don't think that man will come back, but—"

Nick interrupted him as he felt Liza grow even more tense. "I'll be with her."

"Thanks, Doc. Call us if anything comes up."

"I will," he assured him as he stood to escort them to the door. When he closed the door behind them, he turned to look at his patient.

He had a question or two for her. But the exhaustion on her face stopped him. Satisfying his curiosity wasn't as important as her health.

"Time for you to rest, young lady."

Her eyes popped open and she shot him a worried look.

"Don't worry. I'll stay here and keep an eye on you. There's a golf tournament on that I want to see and you just happen to have a big screen TV"

"I— Thank you. I shouldn't be tired," she whispered, "but I am."

"Need me to carry you to bed?" he asked, ignoring her protest.

"No!" she said with a gasp. She pushed herself up from the chair, then wavered.

Nick reached out to steady her. "Okay, just take my arm and we'll stroll to the bed."

She put her hand on his bent arm. He loved the warmth of her near him, her depending on him. You're being foolish, he warned himself. The moment she gets well, she'll be focused on her career again and have no need for you.

But she needed him now.

Liza fell asleep as soon as her head touched the pillow, comforted by the last words she heard the doctor say. He'd keep watch until she woke up.

Five hours later, she stirred, not sure what had awakened her. The late afternoon sun was pouring into the room from the opened draperies. Was that what had bothered her? Or had there been a noise?

Immediately, fear filled her. Was the doctor there? Had that man returned? Or maybe the phone had rung. Maybe Emily had called and she'd missed it.

She sat up in the bed, still tired, but a little more awake.

"Dr. Hathaway?" she called, and waited anxiously for him to open the bedroom door. Relief poured through her when he did. She checked her watch. It was just after four o'clock. She was going to owe him a whopping bill for round-the-clock care.

"How are you feeling?" he asked, smiling at her.

Such a handsome man. It would be easy to have him around, she decided, to look at if nothing else. "Fine. Has anyone called?"

"Nope. Oh, I take that back. Your mother called, but she didn't want to talk to me." He grinned like a little boy who'd done a magic trick. "She hung up."

She couldn't help smiling back. Making her mother disappear would be a magic trick indeed. Cynthia normally traveled with Liza, but she'd been negotiating an appearance on a talk show in Chicago and had left her here in Saratoga Springs.

"Anyone else?"

"Nope. I didn't awaken you for lunch. Are you hungry?" he asked, watching her.

She laughed, her voice a little shaky, still with a huskiness that wasn't normal. "I think all you try to do is fill me up with food."

"Well, so far I haven't done such a good job. You

missed lunch. Why don't you slip on your slacks and we'll go to the restaurant downstairs.''

"No! I mean, I need to be here in case I get any calls," she whispered, avoiding his eyes.

He left the door and walked over to her bed, sitting down on the edge as he'd done in the hospital.

"Before we make any decisions about dinner, I think you'd better answer a question for me."

She supposed she owed him that at least, since he'd done so much for her. With a hesitant nod, she watched him.

"Who is Mrs. Tremble?"

Four

He could feel the tension rise even without touching her. He wanted to assure her to forget his question, that it was important for her to relax. But he also wanted to be sure he wasn't helping her break any laws. So he waited.

"You promised you wouldn't tell," she reminded him.

"I won't help you break the law, Liza."

She shook her head. "I'm not—I wouldn't do that."

"Then answer my question."

She hesitated again. Finally, she said, "I think it's Emily."

"Your cousin? The one you believe was kidnapped? Why didn't you tell the police?'' He frowned at her.

"I…it's complicated.''

"How?''

"I'm not sure it's her, and if it is, I don't know what her situation is now.''

"How could her situation be worsened by the police knowing?'' he asked. "Surely you don't suspect the police would harm her?''

"No,'' she whispered, "but they might make her go back home.''

Her answer gave him pause and raised a lot more questions. "So you think someone in the family caused the problem?''

She shrugged her shoulders and looked away from him.

"Liza, you're not making sense.''

She faced him this time, but her eyes had pools of tears in them. "That's the problem. No one will believe her if—if what I think happened is true. No one.''

"No one but you.''

"Doctor—''

"I think it's time you called me Nick, Liza. We've passed way beyond the doctor-patient relationship.'' More than he wanted, he assured himself. He should just leave, but he couldn't. She was too alone, too defenseless.

"I know I've become a real burden, Nick, and I appreciate all you've done for me.''

"Yeah, well, let's get back to the subject. Why are you the only one who believes this Emily?"

"Because her story doesn't make sense."

Nick gave a heavy sigh and rubbed his face before looking at her again. "Look, Liza, I'm trying to help you, but you're not giving me much to work with."

"You're right," she said with a smile that didn't hold a lot of warmth. Sitting up a little straighter in the bed, she said, "I'm sorry I've taken up so much of your time. I'll call your office and leave an address to mail your bill."

Feeling like the kitten he'd been cuddling had suddenly grown claws, he stared at her. "You want me to leave?"

"I can't explain the situation to you, so I understand why you wouldn't want to be involved."

Frustrated, he stood, shoving his hands in his pockets. "Fine. I'm sure you— Damn it, Liza, what are you going to do? I can't leave you here alone. What if that man comes back? Do you want me to call Detective Ramsey and have him assign a guard?"

"No! I'll—I'll manage on my own."

"Sure! All ninety pounds of you," he growled.

"I weigh more than that," she objected.

"Are you going back to New York?"

Slowly she shook her head, as if making her decisions as they arose with no prior planning. "No, I don't think so."

He studied her, trying to think what to do. Slowly, he said, "I think you should disappear."

"What?"

"If you had a place to go where no one would find you, except Emily, assuming Mrs. Tremble is Emily, that would be best, wouldn't it? Just for a few days."

"But I don't know of anywhere," she said, her voice almost a whisper again.

He sat back down on the edge of the bed. "But I do. Someplace where you'll be safe and have someone to keep an eye on you until you feel better."

"Where?" she asked, frowning.

"My house."

Her green eyes huge, she pushed against the back of the bed, putting as much space between them as possible. "I won't live with you. You've been kind, but I don't— Sex isn't part of the bargain, Dr. Hathaway."

Liza stared at the handsome man sitting beside her, suddenly feeling much more vulnerable. She'd slid off her slacks for her nap. Now she wished she hadn't done so.

His reaction to her words was interesting. Under a light tan, his cheeks were red.

"That's not what I meant!" he assured her.

She lifted her chin and waited.

"I have a housekeeper, Mrs. Allen, and a large house that I'm redoing. There's lots of room, and Bonnie—Mrs. Allen—is always complaining because I don't entertain. You could move into the guest quarters, and she'd have someone to fuss over."

"No, thank you." She kept her response quiet, not wanting to even hint at the response her body was making. It had been a long time since she'd felt any interest in the opposite sex. She'd been engaged once, sure she'd found her true love.

Until her mother had bought him off.

Robert had decided a million dollars in his pocket now was much better than hoping to inherit from her parents one day.

And she'd decided true love was a lot of malarkey and wanted nothing to do with the men in the world. Until Dr. Nick Hathaway had come to her rescue. She wasn't even sure how he'd become so important to her, but the fact that he interested her was warning enough.

"So you're going to go to another hotel? If you're half as well-known a singer as my nurse says you are, you'll be recognized."

"I'll wear a disguise and go under a different name."

"With credit cards that have your real name? How will you pay for anything?"

"I'll get cash from an ATM," she said, jutting her chin out and pressing her lips tightly together.

"That will work for a little while. Except if Mrs. Tremble is your cousin, she'll be calling this afternoon. Where will you tell her you'll be? You don't have much time."

"Stop it! You're—you're being difficult!" she exclaimed in frustration. She knew she was impulsive, not given to advance planning. Her mother ranted about how necessary she was to Liza's career because Liza didn't think ahead.

The problem was her career was more for her mother than her. Now, the kind doctor who had protected her had disappeared and someone who pushed her, just like her mother, had taken his place. He appeared stunned when she said so.

"I'm not— Well, maybe I am, but for your own good."

"That's what my mother says, too." She glared at him.

As if memories of his conversation with her mother came back to him, he frowned, staring at her. Finally, he said, "I didn't mean to upset you. Why don't you get dressed and I'll drive you to my house. Once you meet Mrs. Allen, you won't have any doubts about my intentions."

"I can't leave in case Emily calls," she returned. She really wasn't trying to be obstinate, as her mother often assured her. But the call from Emily was too important.

She sighed with relief when he nodded, as if she'd made sense.

"Then I'll call Bonnie and you can talk to her." He reached for the phone.

"No! I don't want you on the phone in case Emily calls."

"I could go down to my car and get my cell phone, but it really isn't necessary." He dialed zero. "Operator, my friend, Ms. Colton, is expecting an important call. Can you break in if I'm making a local call?" He paused, then added, "Good, thank you."

He hung up the phone and looked at her. "The

operator promises she'll interrupt if a phone call comes in for you. Is it all right if I call my house-keeper now?''

She nodded but couldn't help asking, ''What happens if there's an emergency?''

He pulled back his jacket to show her the beeper on his belt. ''They get my attention this way.''

She noticed that he waited for her approval before he picked up the phone again, leaving the choice up to her. Something her mother never did.

She nodded, not bothering to try to speak. All the talking was making her throat tight again. Besides, if she started talking, she might babble about her gratitude for his behavior. Normal behavior. It would tell him more than any words how difficult her relationship with her mother was.

When someone answered after he'd dialed the number, he greeted the person with warmth. Then he quickly explained that a friend was concerned about causing too much trouble by staying with him. He asked his housekeeper to assure his guest she wouldn't mind. He handed the phone to Liza.

''Hello?'' she said cautiously, her voice still husky.

''Hello, I'm Mrs. Allen, Nick's housekeeper. I'll be delighted to have a visitor. I never have enough to do.''

''But he says—''

''You're a woman!'' the lady exclaimed, interrupting her.

''Yes,'' she said, waiting for the lady's explanation.

"I'm sorry, but it's been so— I mean, we'd love to have you stay with us."

So the doctor had his own secrets? Somehow that made her feel better, though it should've worried her. "Mrs. Allen, I'm a patient of Dr. Hathaway's, not really a friend. I hope that doesn't bother you?"

"Not at all, dearie. It's very quiet here. You'll get a lot of rest. I hope he's told you we're redoing the house. But there's a lull right now in workmen. The recent rains put them behind on their other job and they won't be back for a week or two, so it will be quiet."

"I see. Are you sure you don't mind?"

"Not at all. Will you be— Uh, the guest quarters are quite private."

Liza knew exactly what the woman wanted to know. And she wanted to make sure there were no misunderstandings. "The guest quarters sound perfect, thank you, Mrs. Allen."

"Wonderful. What shall I fix for dinner? Is there anything you don't eat?" The woman's voice was filled with eager enthusiasm.

"Oh, I'm sorry, I have to stay here until after I receive a phone call, so you'd best not count on me for dinner. But I eat just about everything."

Nick reached for the phone, his large, warm hand covering hers. She jerked back from his touch. She'd already discovered she liked it. Too much in the short time they'd been together.

"Bonnie, can you fix up a bed for Liza?"

After a few more details, he hung up the phone. "Okay?"

She nodded. "I'll gladly pay you whatever you—"

"I might have to pay you. Bonnie's so excited about having company. She gets lonesome." He smiled, and a soothing warmth flooded her body.

"I'm sure you're exaggerating." She looked away, not daring to linger in his approval.

"I'll go to the living room. Get dressed and we'll go downstairs to the dining room and have an early dinner while we're waiting to hear from Mrs. Tremble."

"No! They might not—"

"We'll tell the operator to transfer the call there."

He seemed to be back in charge again. But he didn't move to leave the room until she nodded in agreement. A small thing, but it was a big change from her mother's technique.

Nick paced the living area of the suite. What was he doing? Why was he getting involved in this complicated scenario?

Because she was helpless? Beautiful? Because he was bored with life? That thought surprised him. It made him sound a lot like Mrs. Allen. As if prodding a wound, he examined that thought from different angles.

He loved his work, loved helping people. But in actuality, most of his cases weren't all that interesting. Occasionally he traveled to consult with other doctors, but he hadn't had a challenging case in a while. That was okay. He was making people well.

On the other hand, he had no social life. He occasionally played golf with friends. Male friends. But none of them had bothered offering to set him up with a woman in a long time. Maybe because he'd forcefully objected when they'd tried after his divorce.

He'd had dreams of a peaceful life in Saratoga Springs, living with a loving wife, raising a large family, having the life his parents had had. They were both gone now, but he had two brothers and a sister nearby, all raising families.

He was alone, and intended to remain that way. Daphne had cured him of his fantasy expectations about life. The reality was— No, he wasn't that cynical yet. True love existed, he was sure. But maybe not for him.

The rush of adrenaline that had filled him when Liza accused him of asking for sex came back to him. Okay, love might not be a possibility, but obviously sex was. He hadn't lusted after a woman in a while.

Maybe because you hid from life.

He gave a snort of disgust. He didn't need this self-examination right now. Okay, so Liza was beautiful. And, according to his nurse, talented. He was just doing his part to keep culture alive. That was all.

The bedroom door opened.

"Are you dizzy?" he asked abruptly, not liking the paleness of Liza's face.

"No. A little tired, which is ridiculous, but—"

"Recovery takes longer than one good night's

sleep and one nap, Liza. I'm going to call the operator again and transfer any calls to the dining room.''

She nodded and stood, waiting for him to finish. When he did, he pulled a business card from his inside coat pocket and wrote his home number on the back of it. ''Here's the number to give...your caller, if you want to.''

''Thank you,'' she said, stepping forward to take it out of his hand. The urge to pull her to him, to wrap his arms around her, bothered him. But he resisted. Just as he would when he took her to his house. He was a man of his word.

She tucked the card in the pocket of her slacks and picked up her purse. ''I'm ready.''

He took her arm to escort her to the door. Because she might get dizzy, of course. She was still weak.

Once they were seated in the restaurant, almost empty because it was too early for fashionable dining, he explained to the waiter that Liza was expecting an important phone call. The man assured them that he would bring a phone to the table if a call came in.

''Who is Mrs. Tremble?'' he asked.

She looked up, startled. ''I told you—''

''No, I mean, the name had significance for you. How did you know—'' He paused to look around, but no one was close to their table. Before he could explain, she answered his question.

''A doll Emily played with. It was the only toy she brought with her when she arrived at my aunt and uncle's house.''

''They adopted her?''

"Yes, when she was two. Aunt Meredith and Uncle Joe made no difference in treatment between their real children and the others they took in. Theirs was a wonderful house."

He heard the regret and loss in her voice. "You wish you could live there now? Instead of being on tour?"

"No," she said softly, slowly shaking her head. "I may not— That is, things have changed."

The waiter returned to the table with glasses of water and took their order. Liza ordered a chicken Caesar salad. Nick persuaded her to have a cup of soup before her salad, to make sure she had enough to eat. After all, she'd missed lunch.

Then he ordered a steak with a salad and baked potato. He found her staring at him. "Don't tell me you're against steak?"

"No. In fact, I used to enjoy it. But Mother—she generally decides what I eat."

"Why do you let her do that?"

The sadness in her gaze twisted his heart again. What was this woman doing to him?

"I hate to admit it. It makes me sound like a huge wimp."

"Tell me."

"I gave up. It's easier to eat whatever she orders than it is to fight her. I don't really care what I eat anyway."

"She makes a big stink?"

She nodded and took a sip of water.

"But you have the talent. She can't manage without you."

She looked away. "I know, but I don't really have an alternative. I love music. I even enjoy singing. Or I did. Even now, the time on stage is…magical. But the rest of it, the press, the traveling, the pressure. It's getting me down. I thought if I cooperated, my mother would loosen the reins. I was only sixteen when it started. And I'd needed— Aunt Meredith had— I wanted to get away."

Her explanation raised more questions than it answered. Nick had seen her stubborn streak. Why hadn't she shown it to her mother? True, the woman was difficult, but why had Liza given in so easily? Why had she wanted to get away?

He was about to ask that all-important question, when the waiter returned with his salad and Liza's potato soup.

She seemed eager for the soup, and he decided questions could wait. She needed to build her strength.

But he was the only one with that consideration.

She'd only taken a few bites when an older woman stopped at their table, staring at her.

"Are you Liza Colton? You are, aren't you?" she gushed, reaching out to touch Liza.

Nick wanted to stop the woman from touching her, as if such an intrusion would harm her, but Liza smiled and took the woman's hand to give it a gentle shake before withdrawing. "Yes, I am."

"Oh, my dear, I heard you sing the other night. My

husband took me for our anniversary. Oh, I just cried, your voice is so beautiful.''

"I'm glad you enjoyed it," Liza said quietly.

"Oh, my, you sound like you have a cold. What a shame! Can you sing?''

Nick had had all he could stand, even if Liza still had patience. "Ms. Colton is trying to enjoy her dinner. Thank you for stopping by, but she really needs—''

"Oh, of course!" the woman said and Nick breathed a sigh of relief.

Instead of moving on, however, the woman began digging in her large handbag. "Ah! Here's a pen and paper. If I could just get your autograph!" She beamed at Liza, sure her request would be granted.

Not if Nick had anything to say about it. But Liza stopped him with a look just as he started to rise. She quickly signed the paper and smiled again at the lady.

When the woman finally left them, he heaved a sigh of relief. "You were too patient.''

She smiled a small smile. "I know. But she didn't mean any harm.''

"You need to eat while your soup is still warm.''

Without argument, she picked up her spoon and took a bite, leaving Nick to wonder if she was comparing his orders to her mother's. He didn't like that thought. But someone had to take care of her!

They ate in silence, until he couldn't stand it. "Did I sound like your mother? I didn't mean to railroad you, really, but I want you to get your strength back.''

"I know.''

She hadn't answered his question. "Well?"

Looking up, she smiled at him. "No, you didn't sound like my mother. And the soup is good, so I didn't mind."

The waiter interrupted them. "Ms. Colton, you have a call." He handed her a portable phone and walked away.

Nick could tell she tensed as she put the phone to her ear.

"Hello?"

The squawking noise from the phone told Nick at once who had called Liza. He wanted to take the phone from her hand and throw it across the room.

"No, Mother, I'm not well yet. The doctor has insisted on two weeks rest."

More noise.

"No, I'm going to my apartment in New York City, but I'm not going to answer the phone or the door. If it's something important, leave a message. Otherwise, don't call."

Her mother's protest was long and difficult, but Liza listened, not interrupting. Then she said, "Sorry, Mother, but those are the doctor's orders and I'm not going to take a chance with my voice."

More protest.

Then Liza said, "I have to go now, Mother. I'll talk to you in two weeks." She disconnected the phone and waved to the waiter, standing nearby. He came and took the phone away.

She looked at Nick. "Thank you for your excellent orders."

"They really are necessary, Liza. Your voice is sensitive. It needs rest."

"I know," she agreed with a smile. "But I think I sound like Lauren Bacall tonight. Don't you?"

He loved that smile, and her lighthearted response. About to actually flirt with her, much to his surprise, he was interrupted again by the waiter.

"Ms. Colton, you have another call."

If it was her mother again, he was definitely going to throw that phone across the restaurant. But from the look on Liza's face, she wasn't the caller.

Five

Emily Blair Colton almost sobbed with relief when she heard her cousin's voice.

"Liza! It's me!"

"Em, where are you? What's going on? Are you all right?"

Emily blinked back tears. It felt so good to hear the concern, the love, in Liza's voice. "I'm okay. It's been— I'm in Keyhole but don't tell anyone."

Liza gasped. "I'm so relieved!"

"I don't think I've been followed," Emily hurriedly said. Then, after a pause, she added softly, even now feeling like she was betraying someone, "I couldn't go back."

With a sigh, Liza said, "No, of course not, but I'm worried about you."

"It's better here than going back and not knowing. I wouldn't even be able to sleep. Meredith scares me. You know it has to be her." She'd gone over the events time and time again. They didn't make sense—unless one person was behind them—her mother, Meredith Colton.

"You're right," Liza said with a sigh.

"I want you to be careful." Emily took a deep breath. "Don't tell anyone what I told you I suspect. I don't want them coming after you, too."

"Surely they wouldn't— Em, can you describe the man?"

A shudder ran through Emily. Of course she could. She'd seen him in her nightmares for the past three nights. "Yes. He was about forty, skinny except for a potbelly. He has the most ridiculous ponytail, because he's going bald on top. And he has a little beard and a fu-manchu mustache.

"It wasn't him."

"What are you talking about?"

"A man came looking for you...with a knife."

"Oh, Liza, you've got to hide! You mustn't—"

"I'm going to. I was only waiting for your call. But he didn't know where you are. He wanted to know if I'd seen you. The police are looking for him now."

"I'd hoped once they paid the ransom, it would all be over." Emily stifled a sob. "But that's happened, and now this guy shows up. I think you should hide too. At least for a while."

"I am. I have a number where you can reach me."

Emily had the paper on which she'd written the hotel's number. Liza always left her tour schedule with Emily. Thanks to Aunt Cynthia's organizational skills, it hadn't been difficult to find her cousin. "Okay. I'm ready."

After giving her the number, Liza said, "What do you need? Can you come here?"

"That wouldn't be wise if the man knows how close we are," Emily muttered. She'd already thought about going to Liza, but she was sure Cynthia would throw a fit of she interfered with Liza's singing. She knew Liza wouldn't let her down, though. When something mattered, she'd fight her mother tooth and nail.

But Cynthia would alert the family at once.

"I want to send you money," Liza said. "How are you managing?"

Emily didn't want to remember that bizarre, frightening night that started it all. But thank God for Charley Roberts, the trucker who picked her up, fed her and gave her some money. "I'll be all right," she finally said.

"Give me an address and I'll send you plenty of money."

"I can get a job."

"Don't be ridiculous. Just a minute." Emily then heard her voice muffled as she asked for pen and paper.

"Liza? Who's there? You mustn't—"

"Don't worry. He's my doctor. He won't tell anyone."

"Your doctor? Are you sick?" She couldn't bear it if she lost Liza.

"Just a throat problem. I'm almost well. Now, where can I send you money?"

Reluctantly, Emily gave her cousin the post office address of the small Wyoming town of Keyhole where she was hiding.

"I'll wire the money tomorrow, Em. Are you sure you don't want to come here?"

"No. I'm afraid to move. I'm going to get a job here, blend in. I'll be fine."

"Will you call me? Please?"

"Of course. Today's Saturday. I'll call again on Wednesday, about this time, okay?"

"That long? Can't you— Sorry, I know it's difficult. I'll be waiting for your call. Take care of yourself, Emily. I love you."

Emily had never had difficulty with those words, thanks to growing up with Joe and Meredith Colton. They'd shown her what real love, family love, was all about. "I love you too, Liza. Take care of yourself, too. Bye."

Emily collapsed against the side of the telephone booth, tears streaming down her face. Liza was the one person in the world she could count on. Because Liza knew the truth. She couldn't tell Dad. How could she say the woman who'd taken her in, loved her, wasn't the woman bearing her name? No one would believe her.

And she couldn't go back to her beloved home. The

woman she was forced to call Meredith would only try again to get rid of her.

So she was going to hide. With Liza's help.

Nick had watched the powerful emotions on Liza's face as she talked with her cousin. He took the portable phone from her hand and waved the waiter over. "Thanks," he said as Liza surreptitiously wiped her eyes.

When their waiter arrived with their meals, it was a welcome distraction. Nick waited several minutes before he asked, "Is she all right?"

She nodded, but she didn't look at him.

"Liza?"

She lifted her green-eyed gaze and said softly, "She's in hiding. It's dangerous."

He'd recognized her uncle's name, realizing a hefty ransom could be gained from a kidnapping. "Does she think the kidnappers are still after her? After the ransom has been paid?"

Liza dropped her gaze. "Um…yes."

"I think you should—"

"Good evening, Ms. Colton," Detective Ramsey said, stopping beside their table. "Dr. Hathaway," he added with a nod. "May I sit for a moment?"

Nick was afraid Liza would give herself away. Panic was written on her face. "Of course, Detective. May I order you something to drink or eat?"

His question drew the man's attention away from Liza. "I wouldn't mind a cup of coffee," he agreed with a smile.

Nick waved for the waiter as the policeman sat down.

Once the order had been given and the waiter retreated to the kitchen, Nick, after a covert glance at Liza to see she'd composed herself, asked, "Have you found out anything about that man?"

"He bribed the operator here at the hotel. I hope she got a lot because she lost her job."

"Oh, dear!" Liza exclaimed.

Nick had suspected his patient had a soft heart. Her concern for a woman who'd betrayed a trust was evidence of it.

"Don't be concerned for her, Ms. Colton. She knew she shouldn't pass on information," Ramsey said. "But we haven't found anyone who saw him after that, except you two. You haven't seen any sign of him around here?"

"No, we haven't," Nick responded. "But we stayed in Liza's suite all afternoon. She slept."

"You look like you're feeling better," the detective said, looking at Liza.

"Yes, thank you. The sleep helped."

"I understand you had a couple of calls," Ramsey continued, in that easy, nonthreatening style.

Nick tried to keep from tensing, hoping Liza was prepared for the question. While he thought she should tell the police about Emily, he understood her reasoning.

"Yes. My mother called again, and I finally talked to Mrs. Tremble."

"The housekeeper?"

"Yes. She wanted to be sure I was all right."

"And your mother?"

Nick had been watching Liza, admiring her control. But the question about her mother seemed to leave her speechless.

"Her mother wanted to know when Liza would be returning to New York. We were just discussing the possibilities." Nick paused and looked at Liza, before he added, "She's trying to convince me to let her leave this evening."

Liza picked up on his suggestion at once. "I could be in my own bed by nine o'clock. I always sleep better there. And I told my mother I'm going to take a complete rest for two weeks. Not even answer my phone or the door."

"But how would you know if we found out something about your cousin?" Ramsey asked with a frown.

"Anyone with information would leave a message. I could pick up. But I get a lot of calls about my singing career. I don't want to worry about that right now. I need to rest."

"What do you say, Doc?" Ramsey asked, but his gaze was still fixed on Liza.

"I'm considering it. Rest is the most important key to her recovery. If she'll do as she says, I think she might be better off in New York City."

"You know, there's something else I can't figure," Ramsey said, seeming to switch gears.

"What?" Liza asked sharply.

The waiter's arrival with the promised cup of coffee delayed Ramsey's answer.

After taking a sip of the coffee, the detective looked at Liza. "How'd that guy know where to find you?"

"My schedule isn't a secret. My mother's office has the information. All the family, or most of them, have it, also." She frowned. "In fact, he could probably get it off the Internet."

Nick added, "Once he had the city, it wouldn't take many calls to find the right hotel. He'd know that Liza would stay in one of the top hotels."

The detective nodded. "Okay. You want us to notify the NYPD about this suspect so they can keep an eye on you?"

Liza blinked, then smiled that warm smile that lit up her face. "Thank you, Detective, but I don't think so. The FBI will handle the investigation. I'll tell Uncle Joe how helpful you've been, though. I appreciate it."

"Yes, ma'am. Good luck to you." He looked at Nick as he stood. "Thanks for the coffee."

Nick muttered "You're welcome" and watched the man leave the dining room.

"You handled that well," he said softly as he turned back to look at Liza.

"Thank you. And thank you for adding the bit about going back to New York tonight. Do you think he believed me?"

"Yeah. As soon as you finish eating, we'll go check you out and ask them to forward all calls to your apartment. Since you're riding in my car, supposedly to the airport, they won't even be able to trace your movement through a taxi.''

She frowned. ''Maybe I should take a taxi.''

Before he could protest, she added, ''That would keep you from being involved when they discover I didn't board the plane. And you could pick me up.''

He didn't like the idea. He didn't want her out of his sight, but he could see the value of her plan. ''You're pretty good at this hiding thing.''

''Thanks, I think,'' she said with a smile. Then she frowned again. ''But I don't know how to do something else.''

''What?''

''I need to send Emily money without anyone knowing.''

''That's easy. I'll get my accountant to wire the money and you can give me a check that I'll hold until it's safe to deposit it.''

Anxiously she leaned forward. ''But I wanted to send her five thousand dollars. Can you manage—''

Usually women looked at him as a money ticket to their future. Liza doubted his ability to finance her cousin temporarily. He grinned wryly. ''Yeah, I can handle it.''

''First thing in the morning?''

''Yeah, first thing,'' he promised.

She beamed at him. ''Nick, thank you so much. I don't know what I'd do without your assistance.''

He smiled back but he was taking a better measure of his patient. ''Somehow, I think you'd manage.''

"Thank you," she replied, her smile broadening.

"So what I don't understand is why you tolerate your mother." Okay, so it was none of his business. But he'd thought his patient was browbeaten. But with food and rest, she was showing a different side. A strong side. He didn't understand the situation.

If she'd told him his nosiness was rude, or he had no right to ask such a question, he wouldn't have been surprised. But she did neither.

Instead, she ducked her head and murmured, "It's my fault."

"Your fault? Don't be ridiculous. You—"

She looked up and interrupted him. "My mother isn't an easy woman to deal with, but I've encouraged her to be dictatorial."

Nick blinked several times. "I beg your pardon?"

Liza said earnestly, "After I lost the relationship I had with Meredith, I naturally looked toward my own mother. That was a mistake. But at the time I believed we could have that daughter-mother relationship that so many girls take for granted."

She gave a rueful smile that caught Nick's heart.

"I was wrong, but it took several years for me to realize that. By that time, I knew the Meredith I loved had disappeared, either, like Emily believed, through deception, or because of some mental illness." She shrugged. "I was so desperate to replace that feeling, I thought I could have it with my own mother. I decided any kind of relationship with Mother was better than nothing. So I let her have her way."

"And that makes it your fault?" He didn't buy her theory.

She shrugged again. "It's a sin of omission rather than commission, but it's a sin, no less. Lately, I've been trying to change our relationship. Mother's resisted."

They were interrupted by another fan, and Nick ground his teeth. When the woman finally left their table, he said, "Finish your salad and let's get out of here."

With a sigh of relief, she put down her fork. "I'm ready. I didn't want to suggest leaving because I was afraid you'd yell at me to eat more," she said with a teasing look that caught his breath.

"I would, but you're not going to get to eat much now, with all the crowd coming in." He waved to the waiter and signaled for the bill.

"I can sign it to my room," she said.

"No. I'll pay." It was a macho thing, he knew, but he paid nevertheless.

Once they reached her room, he offered to pack for her, but she refused. "I'm an old hand at packing. It won't take me long."

"Why are you traveling alone? Don't most performers have assistants, or maids, or aides or something?" He'd wondered about that.

"I used to have an assistant. But she and Mother didn't get along. Besides, I'm low maintenance. It's easier that way." While she talked, she opened the closet and began removing clothes.

He grabbed her suitcase and lifted it on the bed.

"Thanks." She opened the lid and laid the clothes into the bag, folding them over. Then she moved to the drawers and emptied them. After gathering her belongings from the bathroom, she announced she was ready.

"You *are* fast," he commented, smiling at her.

"Let's get out of here."

He was amused at the fact that she only had one large bag and a small carry-on. His ex-wife had never traveled with less than three bags, even for a weekend.

At the hotel reception, Liza efficiently took care of her bill and graciously accepted the hotel manager's compliments. She didn't forget to tell him she was going to her apartment in New York to recover from her illness, in case anyone inquired after her.

"And is the doctor taking you to the airport?" the manager asked solicitously.

Nick saw the benefit of Liza's plan as she explained that she intended to take a taxi. She didn't want to bother the doctor any more than she had.

The manager immediately offered the use of the hotel limousine, insisting when Liza protested the necessity.

Nick was pleased. He'd worried about letting Liza out of his sight. He'd feel better knowing she was being cared for by one of the hotel employees. When Liza looked at him, he nodded in encouragement.

"Thank you. I appreciate that."

The manager picked up a phone. By the time Liza

had paid her bill, the chauffeur had arrived and took charge of her bag.

Nick walked her to the door of the limo. There, he bent and kissed her cheek, murmuring, "I'll be right behind you."

As she nodded, she said, "Thank you for your excellent care of me, Dr. Hathaway. I'll be sure to tell my mother how helpful you've been." She gave him a brilliant smile and got into the big car.

Nick stood there, watching the limousine drive away.

"She's something, isn't she?" one of the bellboys said, standing near Nick.

He was irritated by the man's comment, but he couldn't disagree. "She sure is."

Liza felt the loss of Nick's comforting presence at once. The cavernous back seat of the limousine, while elegant, only emphasized her isolation.

The driver rolled down the tinted window that divided the car. "Are you returning to New York, ma'am?"

"Yes, I am."

"I'll hurry. The last flight out leaves in forty-five minutes."

"Thank you. I'll appreciate that." His words had her changing her plan. Instead of waiting outside for Nick, she'd have to go inside the airport and pretend to hurry for her plane. She might even buy a ticket. That would keep the police from realizing she hadn't returned to New York for a little while.

The driver would suspect something at once if she lingered.

She hoped Nick would wait.

When they reached the airport, she offered the driver a handsome tip and signaled for a skycap.

"You can check your bags out here," the driver suggested.

"Thank you, but I want to be sure there's a seat left for me before I do that," she improvised. She turned back to the chauffeur. "Thank you again. You've been very helpful."

"My pleasure," he assured her.

She looked over his shoulder, searching for Nick's black Mercedes, but she didn't see it. As she'd planned, she hurried inside to the ticket counter. The reservation clerk assured her there were plenty of seats available. She pulled out a charge card and paid for a ticket. Unfortunately, that meant she had to check her large bag.

"Shall I tag that bag also?" the clerk asked politely, pointing to her smaller bag.

"No, I'll carry it on," she said, her gaze lingering on the large bag as it was placed on the conveyor belt. With a sigh, she silently said goodbye to most of her belongings.

"You'd better hurry to the gate," the clerk warned. "They'll start boarding any minute."

"Thank you," she said with a smile and turned around.

There was a line of people behind her waiting their turn at the counter. Her gaze traveled down the line without even realizing she was doing so. She was turned in the direction of the gates, wondering when she'd be out of sight of the clerk, when a memory forced her to look back.

The second person in line was a big man, looking like his face had been rearranged by numerous fights. And he was wearing a dirty blue shirt. With a gasp, she turned to get out of sight before the man looked for her.

Because she knew he was the one who'd come to the hospital.

The man with a knife.

Six

The Saratoga Springs airport, while small, had all the normal amenities, including traffic. Nick was five cars back of the limo when he first entered the airport, but he fell farther behind as cars whipped in and out, their drivers hurrying to catch flights.

When he finally reached the area where Liza should be, the limo was pulling away from the curb. With a sigh of relief, he pulled to a stop and scanned the sidewalk. When he didn't see her, his heart began thumping louder and panic started to creep in.

Where had she gone? She was supposed to wait for him here. Could she have changed her mind and decided to really go to New York? No, he silently protested. She wouldn't do that.

And if she did, he'd follow her.

That realization, razor sharp with no wavering, told him he'd invested more into Ms. Liza Colton than he'd intended. No, it was only because he was concerned about her as a patient, the doctor in him argued.

He didn't take time to question that statement. The important thing now was to keep Liza safe.

What should he do? If he parked the car, he'd have to go to one of the nearby parking lots. He saw one of the skycaps come out of the building. Putting his car in park, he stepped out and waved to the man.

"Yes, sir," the man said with an ingratiating grin.

Nick reached for his wallet. Since he didn't have any luggage that needed carrying, he'd have to compensate the man for his time.

"I need information," he said, handing the man a ten-dollar bill. "Did you just see a slender brunette get out of a limo?"

The man's eyebrows rose and he studied Nick. Finally, he said, "I might have."

"Did she go in the building?"

"Of course. She had to hurry to make her flight."

Nick's heart fell. Surely she wouldn't leave without telling him. He couldn't believe—

Over the man's shoulder, he saw a white-faced Liza appear in the door, frantically searching for him.

"Thanks," he hurriedly said. He wanted to go to Liza, but he figured the skycap would watch him. When the man's attention was claimed by another traveler, he hurried to his car and opened the back door.

By that time, Liza had seen him and was almost running to the car. He hustled her into the back seat. "Lie down!" he whispered.

He rounded the car and slid behind the wheel just in time, for a policeman was walking toward them. Nick pulled into the traffic immediately.

"Are you all right?" he asked, watching in the rearview mirror.

"Yes, but—but he was there!"

"Who?"

"The man from the hospital!"

"What?" Nick wanted to hit the brakes and reach back for Liza. Her voice was trembling. But the best thing was to get them away from the airport as quickly as possible. "Where?"

"He was the second person in line behind me. He had a baseball cap on with his hair hidden beneath and he wore the same blue shirt. I'm sure it was him."

"Did he see you?"

"I'm sure he did. That's why he was in line. He was buying a ticket to New York, too. But he didn't watch me walk away. I think he assumed I was going to the gate." Her voice was still breathless, but he could hear a weariness creep in.

"You bought a ticket to New York?"

"The chauffeur told me the last flight was in forty-five minutes and I had to hurry. I couldn't stand outside waiting for you, so I decided if I bought a ticket it might cover my tracks better."

Nick breathed more easily. She hadn't planned to

run away from him. A good thing, too, since the man had been watching for her.

"Is anyone following us?" she asked, sounding even more tired.

Nick looked in the rearview mirror. There was a minivan behind, and he could see several children inside. A stretch limo, much like the one she'd ridden in, pulled alongside, then passed them.

"No, there's no one around us, except a family. But I think you should stay down anyway. We don't want anyone to see you with me." When she didn't answer, he risked a look over his shoulder. Her eyes were closed, her breathing even.

She'd gone to sleep.

It was amazing she hadn't collapsed earlier, considering her physical condition and the long day she'd had. Of course, she'd had a lengthy nap, but the body didn't snap back all that quickly when it wasn't receiving the proper nutrients or rest.

He picked up his car phone and called home. "Bonnie? You might prepare some kind of dessert or snack for our guest. I'm bringing her home now."

"I have a chocolate pie I baked this afternoon, just in case," Mrs. Allen assured him.

He wasn't sure in case of what, but he wasn't going to complain. "Good. Oh, and Bonnie? You can't tell anyone we're having a guest."

"Why?"

"I'll explain when we get there."

When strong arms encircled her, Liza snuggled in close, enjoying the security she felt, without ever opening her eyes. She vaguely remembered something scaring her, but she felt safe now.

Movement began to rouse her, reluctantly. A bright light did the rest. She slowly opened her eyes, blinking at the change. "What... Oh! Dr. Hathaway!"

"I thought you were going to call me Nick?" he asked, his voice soft, but she heard it rumble through his chest.

"Is she sick?" someone else asked.

Liza lifted her head, realizing she had her arms around the doctor's neck as she did so. "No, I fell asleep," she assured the woman, turning toward her.

Nick's housekeeper was older, maybe as old as sixty, but she wore a warm smile that lit up her pale blue eyes. She was dressed in a comfortable housedress, her rounded form motherly.

"Liza, this is my housekeeper, Mrs. Allen. Bonnie, this is Liza. She's going to stay with us for a while."

Liza noted that he didn't give her last name. He probably thought his housekeeper wouldn't recognize her.

"Liza Colton, as I live and breathe!"

"You know who she is?" Nick asked, startled.

Liza said nothing as he put her feet on the floor. There had been a lot of publicity about her performances. Her mother was good at that.

"A'course I do. I even heard she was sick and had to cancel her last show. Are you all right, lovey?"

"I'm getting better," Liza said, noting that the huskiness in her voice had returned. "Just a little tired."

Her gaze turned to Nick's face as she added that last. He was frowning.

"After you eat a snack, you're going straight to bed."

"Eat? But I had dinner."

"That was a couple of hours ago. Bonnie has made her famous chocolate pie. You'll eat a piece of it."

Chocolate pie was the best medicine a doctor had ever prescribed for her, so she nodded.

"Maybe you should get dressed for bed and I'll bring the pie to your room," Mrs. Allen offered, beaming at Liza.

Liza began to smile, liking the picture the woman had drawn, when she suddenly realized its flaw. "I don't have any clothes!"

Nick and Mrs. Allen stared at her.

"But your suitcase—" Nick began.

"Is on its way to New York," Liza finished, discouragement in her voice. "I have my makeup bag, my toothbrush, comb and brush. Shampoo and all that stuff. But no clothes."

"Damn! I hadn't thought of that."

Mrs. Allen gave Nick a strange look. Then she reached out and patted Liza's shoulder. "Don't you worry. Sit down and eat a piece of pie, and we'll find you something to sleep in. First thing tomorrow Nick can buy you some new clothes."

Liza sat down, glad to do so. Her legs still weren't strong.

Nick, with his fists cocked on his waist, looked at

Mrs. Allen. "Tomorrow's Sunday. There won't be many stores open until the afternoon."

"The bargain stores will be. You can just pick up a few things and let her find more clothes later."

"No! No, she can't go out shopping."

"But, Nick," Liza began in protest. But he stopped her.

"You can't be seen, Liza. Even Bonnie recognized you, and she doesn't pay all that much attention to the comings and goings of celebrities. We can't take that chance."

He paused before adding, "And you need to call the airline and ask them to collect your suitcase in New York and hold it for you because you took another flight."

She suddenly remembered what had frightened her earlier. That man at the airport. The one who was looking for Emily. And had come into her room with a knife.

Now she wished she'd never remembered.

Nick saw her shudder. The stress and exhaustion were taking their toll. She needed rest and it was up to him to make sure she got it.

"I'll pour her a glass of milk while you cut the pie," he told his housekeeper, which got her moving. He did as he'd said and put the milk in front of Liza.

"You're always giving me milk to drink," she said, a plaintive note in her voice.

"I can make you some—"

"No," Nick said, interrupting Bonnie. "She needs

to drink milk until she gets stronger. I want her to have milk at every meal.''

Both ladies looked exasperated with him, but he didn't care. He was Liza's doctor, and it was his responsibility to get her well. To protect her. He wanted to pull her back into his embrace and promise her no one would scare her again.

The memory of holding her in his arms as he carried her into the house warmed him. She didn't weigh much. But what there was of her packed a strong sensual punch. He hadn't hungered after a woman like this since the first days of his marriage to Daphne. Before he'd realized what she was.

"I'll have some coffee," he said as he opened a cabinet and took out a mug. "You want some, Bonnie?"

After an uncertain look at their guest, his housekeeper said, "I'll drink a little milk."

"Oh, no!" Liza protested. "It's all right if you have coffee. I like milk."

"Are you sure?" Bonnie asked anxiously.

That smile that always warmed his insides appeared on Liza's beautiful face. "He's a tyrant, but it's for my own good."

Bonnie gave a satisfied nod before she told Nick she'd take coffee, too. Then she brought three pieces of pie to the table.

The cozy threesome chatted lightly while they ate. Nick was grateful his housekeeper didn't ask any of the questions he was sure she had in mind. He didn't want anything to disrupt Liza's sleep when she finally got to bed.

When he signaled it was time for Liza to go upstairs, she looked at the two of them. "If either of you have a T-shirt I could borrow, I could sleep in that."

"Of course, you can have a T-shirt," he said at once, trying not to think about one of his shirts sliding down her silken skin.

Bonnie added, "I might even be able to find some—undergarments that Nick's wife left behind. There's a box in the storage room." She ignored Nick's stare.

He didn't realize there were any of Daphne's things still there. "There are?"

"Nick's wife?" Liza repeated.

He met her wide-eyed green gaze.

"I was married. I'm not now." He hadn't meant to sound so curt, but he didn't want to discuss the miserable years he'd shared with Daphne.

Instead of asking any questions, Liza looked at Bonnie.

"Don't mind him," she said with a smile. "He's touchy, but he doesn't mean any harm."

Feeling the women had closed ranks on him, Nick pushed away from the table. "I'll get a T-shirt." He hurried from the room.

When he returned to the kitchen, he found it empty. Assuming Bonnie had escorted Liza to the guest wing of the old house, he went back upstairs and turned right.

He tapped on the only door in the hallway that was closed.

Bonnie opened the door. "Oh, good. She's really tired."

"Yes. After she changes and gets into bed, I want to see her." He told himself he wanted to check her pulse. But he knew he also just wanted to see her again, to be sure she was all right. He'd stay with her until she fell asleep. As her doctor.

"I'll tell her," Bonnie promised and promptly closed the door in his face.

When she opened it five minutes later, he was leaning against the wall, patiently waiting.

"Oh! I was going to call you," she pointed out, staring at him.

"I waited," he said unnecessarily. Then he pushed past her. "I'll be down in a minute." He hoped Bonnie understood that he didn't want her to wait with him. He guessed he'd made himself clear when she headed down the hallway.

He entered the room, finding Liza propped up by several pillows, the covers pulled high on her chest. He could still see the white cotton of his T-shirt, though.

"How are you feeling?"

"Tired," she said, a soft smile on her full lips.

He sat down on the edge of the bed and picked up her wrist, checking her pulse. "You took your antibiotic, didn't you?"

"Yes, I did. I'm glad I didn't pack them in my suitcase, or they'd be in New York now."

"And you called the airline about your luggage?"

"Yes, they were very helpful," she assured him, that soft smile still on her lips.

He wanted to kiss those lips, to wrap his arms around her slim body, to slide under the covers and strip her of his own T-shirt. The strength of those urges surprised him. He stood and moved to a small chair nearby. "Go to sleep. I'll wait until you do."

She didn't say anything, but her smile was enough. He basked in it even after her eyes closed. Almost immediately, her breathing evened out and she was asleep.

He wondered if she always fell asleep so easily, the supposed sign of a clear conscience, or if it was because of her medical condition.

He had a million questions about her. And in spite of the fact that he'd called her a diva in his mind, he wanted to hear her sing. Not yet. When she'd recovered. Somehow, he knew her voice would be incredible.

Which meant she was gifted, and that gift would require that she eventually leave.

That was the one thing Nick didn't want to think about.

When Liza woke up, sunshine was peeking through the blinds that covered the windows. She stretched, reluctant to get up. Checking her watch, she sat bolt upright—it was almost noon.

Mrs. Allen would think she was lazy. Shoving back the covers, she discovered bare legs, topped by a soft white T-shirt. Then she remembered she had no clothes.

Before she got too discouraged, she discovered several packages on the chair where she'd last seen Nick. Upon investigation, she found panties, several bras, a pair of jeans, some khaki slacks and two blouses and a sweater.

She hurriedly dressed, finding everything perfectly sized. She wondered how Nick had known until she remembered last evening Mrs. Allen had carried away her clothes to wash them. She must've given Nick the proper sizes.

With her stomach growling, Liza hurried down the stairs, hoping she'd find the housekeeper in the kitchen.

"Good morning, lovey," Mrs. Allen greeted her with a big smile. "How are you this morning?"

"Very rested but feeling guilty for sleeping so long."

"No need for that. Nick said you hadn't been sleeping well. You're just catching up. Sit down and I'll fix you some breakfast."

Basking in the motherliness of Mrs. Allen, Liza slid into a chair. "Just some toast, please. Nick will make me eat a full lunch and it's almost lunchtime."

"That he will. That boy will make a fine father one day, won't he?"

Liza's smile faltered momentarily, but she regrouped and nodded in agreement.

"Want some orange juice instead of milk since the

tyrant isn't home?'' Mrs. Allen asked, seemingly having noticed nothing.

"Oh, I'd love some orange juice."

Soon she was munching warm buttered toast smeared with strawberry preserves and sipping juice. She wanted to ask where Nick was, but she decided it was none of her business.

Her patience paid off, however. Mrs. Allen volunteered the information.

"Nick decided to go on to church like normal this morning. He figured it would look better. Then he said he might try one of the local department stores to buy you more clothes."

"Oh, no! I mean, he's bought me plenty. I can manage with these things. And they fit really well." They were roomy, but so were her own clothes after this past week.

"That boy is hardheaded, lovey. If he thinks you need more clothes, he'll buy them, regardless of what you say. He's very protective."

"Yes," Liza said fervently. "He's done so much for me."

"Did you come to him about your throat?"

Liza realized she'd done so only two days ago, but it seemed so much longer. "Yes. I—I hadn't been sleeping or eating as I should and my voice collapsed— My voice!" she exclaimed, suddenly realizing she sounded like her normal self. She beamed at the housekeeper. "My voice is back."

"It may not be as strong as it was. Nick is always saying it takes time to recover."

"Yes, I know, but it's such a relief to sound normal."

"Were you worried about never singing again?"

Liza thought about her question. "Professionally, you mean?"

Mrs. Allen nodded. "It must be grand to know that your voice can bring an entire audience to its feet, cheering."

Liza frowned. "Yes, I suppose. But frankly, I've grown a little tired of performing. You have to be constantly on the road, traveling. I never get to see my family. My cousin Em— My cousin and I are very close, and we only get to see each other three or four times a year."

"A girl cousin?" Mrs. Allen asked, her voice sharp.

"Why, yes."

"I imagine a pretty girl like you has a lot of men around her."

Liza gave her a rueful smile. "You haven't met my watchdog mother. The only man I thought I cared about was bought off because Mother feared he'd ruin my career." With a sigh, she added, "I don't think she had anything to worry about since he was obviously only marrying me for my money. He would've pushed me to sing as much as Mother."

"Your mother paid him off?" Mrs. Allen asked, scandalized. "Well, I never! Don't you worry, lovey, as pretty as you are, you'll find a man to love you."

Before Liza could answer, with what she didn't know, they both heard the garage door open and Nick call out, "I'm home. Anybody here?"

Seven

Nick found Liza and Bonnie in the kitchen. He wasn't sure what was going on when he discovered Liza's cheeks a bright red and her green eyes wide as she stared at him. Bonnie, on the other hand, was beaming with approval.

"What's up?"

"Nothing!" Liza hurriedly replied.

"We're waiting for you to return so I can serve lunch," his housekeeper said. "Did you go shopping?"

"Yeah." He avoided looking at Liza. He'd found the shopping strangely intimate. Picturing Liza in the clothes he bought had been unsettling enough. But when he'd moved to the lingerie department, those mental pictures had become X-rated. "I left the packages in the laundry room."

"Well, bring them in!" Bonnie exclaimed. "I'm sure Liza is eager to see what you selected."

"No!" Liza exclaimed. She didn't look at him. "You've already bought me enough. See, I'm wearing them."

"Very nice. But I don't think two changes of clothes will do for two weeks. You'd wear them out by constantly washing them. Besides," he added, "those clothes aren't nice. I'm sure you're used to more elegant outfits, more expensive fabrics." He knew it. Wealthy women didn't dress in plain clothes. Daphne had spent large sums on her clothes, each outfit costing more than a family's monthly food bill.

"Oh, you're too slow," Bonnie said and rushed from the room.

Surprised, Nick protested, but it was too late. He'd intended to leave the boxes with the silk underwear until he could deliver them to Liza's room. The picture in his mind of a private fashion show made him forcefully shut it down. That wasn't what he meant.

But it was a wonderful fantasy.

"Nick?"

"Uh, yeah?" he asked, pulling himself together.

"Did you wire the money?"

"Yeah. I talked to my accountant early this morning. He promised to take care of it at once."

"Thank you. If you'll tell me the total you spent, I can write a check for the money order and the clothes together."

"No need. I charged everything. I won't get the bill for a month." He didn't want her to pay for the clothes. He liked providing for her, though he didn't ask himself why.

"My," Bonnie exclaimed, coming back into the room with her arms full. "You really got carried away. Come on, Liza. Let's look at what Nick chose. He has wonderful taste."

Without waiting for Liza to join her, Bonnie put the pile of boxes down on the kitchen counter and lifted the lid from the first box.

Nick groaned as he realized she'd found the one box he didn't want opened. The pale lime silk bra and panties were on top. When he'd seen the color, unusual for lingerie, he'd immediately pictured Liza, with her green eyes, in a sultry pose.

"I, um, I thought you might need more underwear."

"What woman wouldn't need this?" Bonnie exclaimed. "Look, Liza, there's three more sets, each in a different color. Peach, blue and white, too. Aren't they lovely?"

"Lovely," Liza said faintly.

The next box revealed two Dior nightgowns, simple in design in a silky material that was opaque but thin. With matching robes.

Nick had had about all he could take. He scooped those two boxes off the counter and put them in a chair, out of sight beneath the table. "The other boxes are clothes. I hope you like them."

Liza gave him an uncertain look.

Did she think he was trying to seduce her? That he wouldn't keep his word? He'd promised not to touch her—and he hadn't. He hadn't promised not to fantasize about her, though.

Bonnie opened a box to show Liza a cashmere sweater in forest green, with a matching slim wool skirt. Since the October air already had a chill in it, it was a perfect outfit for a day outing.

"But—but if I can't go out, I won't need an outfit like that."

He shrugged. "You can wear it later."

He'd made other purchases, more casual. A denim jumper with several blouses to wear with it. A navy suit by Chanel. A long-waisted plaid wool dress with white cuffs that would make Liza look about eighteen. Corduroy pants in tobacco brown and a thick cream-colored sweater that would fall to her thighs.

"This is too much, Nick," Liza protested.

Daphne had never stopped shopping, though she'd had several closets stuffed full. Had he been testing Liza? That thought hadn't occurred to him until that moment. If he had been, however, Liza had passed with flying colors.

"It's not much, Liza. And if you need something else, just let me know." He cleared his throat. "Our shopping here is almost as good as New York's."

A bold statement, but even Daphne had considered the shopping excellent. Saratoga was a popular resort for the wealthy of New York, especially in racing season.

"I'm sure it is."

"I told you Nick had excellent taste. Now, you two take these things upstairs and put them away while I get lunch on the table. Because I suspect Nick will want you to take a nap right after," Bonnie predicted, still smiling.

"But I just woke up," Liza protested.

"Maybe we'll watch a little football instead." He figured that would put her to sleep without even trying. Most women didn't like football.

"Who's playing?" she asked, surprising him.

"Uh, I know the Giants and Cowboys are playing in one game. I'm not sure about the second game."

"Oh, then let's hurry." She grabbed half the boxes and hurried out the door.

Nick stared at his housekeeper. "She likes football?"

"Sounds like it to me. You're a lucky man."

Bonnie watched her employer hurry from the room, carrying the elegant clothes he'd purchased.

Things were turning out very well.

She'd been surprised when Nick had called to say they were having a guest. He seldom entertained— and never women. So she'd assumed he was having a friend or colleague, a man, visit. She'd been shocked to discover him with a woman in his arms. And thrilled.

Then she'd realized the woman was famous, wealthy and beautiful and her elation took a nose dive. Too similar to Daphne, the horrible woman he'd divorced.

But Liza didn't act like Daphne. She'd been more

than agreeable so far. Not at all demanding. Apologizing for sleeping late. Not condescending to the "help" as Daphne had been.

Even better, Nick's choice of clothes for his guest had been quite revealing, in several ways. Bonnie grinned as she again pictured the underwear—and Nick's red cheeks as she'd held them up for Liza to see.

It had been four years since he and Daphne had parted ways. It was unnatural for a man to go that long without female companionship. Bonnie had begun to worry about him.

But it was plain to see that Liza made his temperature rise.

Good.

Now it was time to help things along.

Liza told Nick she'd put away the clothes later. She didn't seem to want to do so in front of him. She suggested they shouldn't keep Mrs. Allen waiting.

While he suspected her reasons were more than that, he agreed and followed her back downstairs. They entered the kitchen to find three trays lined up on the kitchen counter.

He stared at them.

"Hurry up, Nick," Bonnie ordered.

He stared at her.

"I thought you'd want to eat in the den so you wouldn't miss any more of the game. It's been on for half an hour already."

Since his housekeeper insisted he eat each meal at

the table, claiming television ruined a man's digestion, Nick was more than justified in his surprise. Liza, however, didn't realize Mrs. Allen was making a radical change.

"That's very thoughtful of you, Mrs. Allen. You must be a football fan, too," Liza said, smiling sweetly.

"Oh, my, yes, lovey. I do enjoy my football. Now, I'll get the pot roast out of the oven while you serve yourselves some salad and hot rolls. Then, we'll finish off the chocolate pie for dessert."

Now Nick was really suspicious. Unless Bonnie had hidden it well, he'd never seen her watch football. He wasn't even sure she knew who the Giants were. She was up to something. Maybe she'd read his mind about Liza falling asleep.

Assuming that was it, he smiled in agreement and served Liza salad. She offered him the plate of hot rolls. When Bonnie set a large pot on the stove and removed the lid, the fragrant scent of slow-cooked beef filled the room.

"Mmm, I think my appetite is returning, Bonnie. Your cooking would tempt a saint," Liza said with a smile, bringing pleasure to his housekeeper.

Not once in the five years he and Daphne were married had he seen Mrs. Allen respond like that. Of course, not once in those years had his wife ever complimented the housekeeper for her excellent work.

"Help yourself, lovey."

Liza did just that, taking a healthy serving of the

pot roast and the potatoes, carrots and onions that accompanied it.

While they'd been filling their plates, Bonnie had filled glasses with iced tea. Nick had conceded to allow Liza to drink her milk with dessert.

"Can you carry your tray, Liza?" Nick asked.

"Of course I can," she replied indignantly. "I'm not a child."

"No, but you're not at full strength." Since he carried her in last night, he didn't think she could argue with that evaluation. She opened her mouth to do so, however.

"Now, no arguing. You're missing part of the game," Mrs. Allen warned, as if the game was the most important event in the world.

But it did the trick. Liza put a glass of tea on her tray and lifted it. Then she looked around in surprise.

"What is it?" he asked.

"I don't know where the den is. I've only seen the kitchen and my bedroom."

"Sorry. I'll work in the fifty-cent tour later. Follow me."

The den was his favorite room in the house. Large windows covered one wall, looking out on the woods that lined his backyard. A big-screen television was on the other wall and several large green plaid couches, both soft and cushiony, faced it.

He set his tray on the coffee table and opened a nearby closet to extract three snack tables. Unfolding one for Liza at the end of one sofa, he stood back for her to set down her tray. Once she was settled, he unfolded his table beside hers, then Bonnie's in front of the other sofa.

"You don't mind, do you? I can see the television better from here," he said, sitting down beside her.

"No, of course not, but maybe I should take the other place so Bonnie can have a good seat. She seemed very enthusiastic."

"She can see fine from over there. Or were you teasing about liking football?"

"No, I love it. Uncle Joe and the boys liked to play touch football. They always roped us girls into playing, too."

"You? You played touch football? Did you get hurt a lot?"

"Nope. They couldn't catch me. I'm very fast," she claimed, a big smile on her face.

Even as he watched, the smile disappeared. "Those were wonderful years."

"You sound like they're lost forever."

"They are," she said with a finality that told him she didn't want to discuss her family. "Are you going to turn on the game?"

He stood and reached for the remote control just as Bonnie came to the door without her tray. "Children, if you don't mind, I've decided to give the game a miss today. I'd forgotten about a murder mystery I began last night. I'm dying to find out who the killer is."

"I could tell you," Nick offered. He'd recommended the book to Bonnie after reading it himself.

"Don't you dare! You don't mind, do you, Liza?"

"Of course not, Bonnie, if that's what you want."

"Good. You cheer on those, uh, midgets for me." With a smile, the housekeeper disappeared.

Liza shot a puzzled look at Nick. "Midgets?"

"I think she means Giants."

After staring at him, Liza said, "She doesn't watch football, does she?"

"Not that I know of," he confessed.

"Then why did she say she did?"

"I think she was trying to make you feel welcome."

"Oh, what a dear. You're very fortunate to have her, Nick."

"I couldn't agree more," he assured her. Not only was Bonnie an excellent cook, she made his house a home, taking the place of his dead parents. And she was apparently determined to do the same for Liza.

Nick was pleased.

Several hours later, Liza stretched, her lashes fluttering open. She didn't move, however, being too comfortable to rush the waking up.

Until she heard a heart beat under her ear. Her eyes opened wide and she realized she was leaning on Nick, using him as her pillow. His arm was wrapped around her, but his gaze was on the television.

"I'm sorry," she said, pushing away from his warm body. "You must be stiff from having to hold me. You should've wakened me."

"Why? I was planning on you sleeping."

"But— You tricked me, Nick Hathaway!"

"Not guilty, Liza Colton. I didn't lure you to sleep. I just offered the opportunity. You're the one who closed your eyes—smack dab in the middle of the game you professed to love."

"I do enjoy it. I guess I was just more tired than I expected. I'm eating and sleeping all the time, it seems. When will I be back to normal?" If that were possible while Nick was around. Just looking at him caused her pulse to race, and made her want to dive back into his comforting embrace.

"In a couple of weeks. But you'll need to take it easy even then. Do you have singing dates scheduled?"

"I told Mother to cancel everything for the next four weeks, to give myself plenty of time. I don't want to try to concentrate on performing while Emily is still in trouble."

He nodded. He'd asked very few questions about her conversation with Emily, for which she'd been grateful. She wasn't sure it was wise to tell anyone, even him.

"Ready for your chocolate pie?"

To her surprise, she was. "You know, I think I am." She laughed. "I'm going to have to go on a diet when I leave here."

Nick instantly frowned. "I want no talk of diets, young lady. Eat sensibly, that's the key."

"Does sensible eating include chocolate pie?"

"It's part of a healthy variety," he assured her.

When she started to rise as he did, he put a hand

on her shoulder, easing her back onto the sofa. "I'll bring it. You rest."

They'd almost finished their pie and milk when the phone rang. Nick picked up the portable resting on the coffee table and answered.

"Dr. Hathaway, this is Detective Ramsey."

With a warning look in her direction, Nick said, "Yes, Detective. How are you?"

Liza pressed her ear close to the receiver so she could hear the conversation.

"Fine. Did you take Ms. Colton to the airport?"

Nick said calmly, "No, I didn't. The hotel offered to send her in a limo." He winked at Liza. "You know how these stars are. She took them up on it at once. Is there a problem?"

"I'm not sure. We tried to contact her at the number she gave us. Left a message, but she hasn't contacted us."

"She was quite tired. She may sleep for hours at a time. But I thought you'd wrapped up your investigation."

"We had reports of a man similar to her description at the airport. The security guards called us. We wanted to make sure she arrived home safely."

"I see. I thought maybe you'd heard something about her cousin."

Dead silence followed his statement.

"Why would you ask that?" the detective roughly demanded.

Liza shot a startled glance at Nick, who was frowning.

"I'm not sure. You have, haven't you?"

More silence. "We just need to know where Ms. Colton is."

"Why?" Nick demanded.

"I don't think that's any of your business, Doctor, unless you know something about Ms. Colton that you're not telling me. I'd hate to have to arrest you, a respectable doctor, for interfering in a police investigation."

"All I know is Liza talked about disappearing for a few days because she was frightened by that man. I assumed that's what she meant when she told her mother she wouldn't answer her phone or the door."

"Do you have a phone number for her mother?"

Nick chuckled. "You've obviously never talked to the woman. No one would do so willingly." Then he winced as Liza elbowed him in the ribs.

"What do you mean?"

"Let's just say she's not an easy woman to talk to."

"What about Ms. Colton's home in California?"

"Detective, I was her doctor—and only briefly. Her New York apartment number is all I have. I suppose you could call her Uncle Joe, Joe Colton. Maybe she contacted him."

Liza shook her head violently. She didn't want Uncle Joe worrying about her, and she couldn't call him from here to reassure him. The number might show up on his caller ID.

The detective sighed in frustration. "Look, I need

some advice and you spent the most time with the lady.''

"You mean Ms, Colton?''

"Yeah, Ms. Colton.'' Detective Ramsey sounded annoyed. "Do you think she and her cousin might've concocted this whole setup?''

Liza was even startled by the detective's question, and her indignant gaze shot to Nick. He slightly shook his head. "Absolutely not. Ms. Colton's medical condition stemmed from the shock of her cousin's disappearance and her consequent lack of sleep and food. No one would do that to herself.''

"I've heard of stranger things. And if that's true, how come she's doing so much better? Unless she's heard from her cousin and didn't tell anyone.''

Liza feared Nick had painted himself into a corner.

But he calmly answered, "She's doing better because I sedated her enough that her body took over while her mind was shut down. I probably should've kept her here longer, because she may reverse her recovery. But I couldn't legitimately detain her.''

"Hmmm.''

"Why would you think that anyway, Detective?''

"For a pretty good reason, Doctor. Mr. Colton received a phone call—from her apartment.''

"He did?'' Nick repeated.

Liza was stunned. Why would someone call from her apartment unless...he'd broken in.

Eight

Nick stared at Liza's stunned expression even as he held the phone. Then, without consulting her, he said, "Detective, I think it would be a good idea if we spoke in person. Can you come to my house?"

After a tense silence, the detective said, "Yeah. When's convenient?"

"I know it's Sunday, but I think now would be a good time."

"Me, too. I'll be there in twenty minutes." Detective Ramsey hung up without saying goodbye.

"Nick! What are you doing? He'll figure out I'm here. You promised to hide me, not show me off to the police!" Panic was in her voice as she shoved away from him.

"You're not thinking, honey," he said quietly. "If

we don't let them know you've been here all along, that you didn't make that call, the investigation is going to get off-track. And, frankly, I'm not interested in being arrested.''

"Okay, then, I'll pack and disappear.'' She leaped from the couch, obviously putting her words into action.

Nick grabbed her hand, holding her back. "You don't need to do that. It won't hurt for the police to know where you are. They'll keep it secret.''

"From my family? I don't think so.''

She had a point. But he still thought he'd done the right thing. "You'll have to explain to the detective why your family can't know.''

"How can I do that?'' she cried, frustration and anger in her voice. Even with the stress she was under, Nick noted that her voice was pure and beautiful.

"Tell him why.''

"It doesn't make sense, Nick. No one will believe me. He'll know I talked to Emily, and—I can't betray her.''

"No, he won't. You suspected your aunt from the beginning, didn't you?''

"Maybe. I knew things weren't right and Emily confirmed it. Kidnapping her wasn't the goal. And killing her didn't make sense unless it was Aunt Meredith, or whoever the woman is.''

"You think killing was the motive? But the ransom note? What about that?'' he asked, staring at her.

"Emily— She said the man was trying to kill her.''

Nick frowned. "Maybe you could not mention that

you think it was attempted murder. Just tell the detective that you suspect someone in the family is involved. That won't be a big surprise. It's frequently the case where a victim knows the perpetrator of a crime." He ran his hands up and down her arms to calm her.

Unfortunately, that action had a reverse effect on *him*. It had been difficult enough to hold her against him while she slept, knowing she trusted him to hold her and not take advantage of her. Now, with her awake, intensely involved in their conversation, the urge to take her in his arms again, to kiss her soft lips, to claim her, for at least a while, was strong.

"Let me go, Nick. I need to get out of here. You haven't given me enough time to—"

"If you go, you'll be in danger, Liza. You can't go to your apartment. The man will be watching it."

"Why do you think that?"

"Who do you suppose made the phone call from your apartment?"

She sank back onto the couch. "Oh, mercy, I hadn't thought of that. You think he was there? But I have a doorman. He wouldn't let anyone in my apartment. He couldn't have— But who—" She closed her eyes, as if she couldn't face the reality of what he was saying. "What if I'd really gone home?" she muttered, her voice rising.

Nick didn't pull his punches. She had to understand how serious her situation was. "You might be dead by now."

Her face paled. "And maybe Emily, too," she

whispered. "He might have been able to force me to tell him."

"Yeah."

To his surprise, she threw herself into his arms. "Oh, Nick, thank you for bringing me here. You saved my life!"

He held her against him and dropped a kiss on her temple. The thought of anyone harming the beautiful woman in his arms was horrifying. As was the possibility of her not being in his life. He drew her across his lap and held her close.

After several minutes, she pushed away from his chest. "I have to tell them, don't I?"

"Just where you are and why you tried to hide. Even if the detective doesn't believe your reasons, I think he'll keep your whereabouts secret. But he can reassure your uncle that you're safe without giving away your location."

"I hadn't thought about worrying Uncle Joe. Not really. I thought he'd believe I was resting in my apartment."

"I'm sure someone has already told him the call came from your apartment. He must be beside himself with worry." Nick pulled her back against him, wrapping his arms around her again, unable to resist the temptation. "I know I would be," he muttered.

She struggled from his arms and stood. "I shouldn't have thrown myself at you. I'm sorry."

"I promised I wouldn't make demands on you, Liza. I keep my promises," he assured her. He'd die if she became afraid to be alone with him.

"All the more reason I shouldn't— It wasn't fair of me to take advantage of you."

"I'm not a teenager, Liza. In fact, you'll consider me quite old. I'm thirty-eight, twelve years older than you. I do have some self-discipline." He wouldn't tell her how weak that self-discipline seemed to be since she'd come into his life.

She nodded but took another step back, as if she could read his thoughts in his eyes.

"Too old for you?" he asked ruefully, wondering if she had any idea what he was asking.

"No! No, you aren't too old for anything. And I appreciate your honesty." Her voice was breathy, as if she'd been jogging.

Before he could respond, the doorbell rang.

He looked at his watch. "Either Detective Ramsey is faster than he said, or we have another caller. You stay here and don't make any noise."

Leaving her standing beside the couch, he closed the door behind him and hurried to the front door, not wanting Bonnie to be involved in what was going on. Detective Ramsey stood on the porch.

He opened the door. "You're quicker than you said," he pointed out even as he invited him in.

"There was no traffic," the man said, his gaze razor-sharp as he stared at Nick.

Nick knew he'd hurried because he was afraid something might happen before he could get here. He didn't blame the detective. Left to Liza, that was exactly what might have happened.

"This way," Nick said, not bothering to explain anything.

He opened the door to the den. But Liza wasn't standing by the couch anymore. For a second, his heart clutching, Nick thought she might've run, as she'd wanted.

Then he saw her standing behind the door. The detective wasn't far enough into the room to see her. Nick stood aside to wave him in. Then he closed the door and took Liza's hand.

"Detective Ramsey, I lied to you on the phone, as you can see. Liza is here, and has been here since last evening."

The detective stared at Liza. "So I see."

Nick tugged on Liza's hand, pulling her with him to the first sofa. "If you'll sit down, I think we can explain our reasons."

"I hope so, or I'll be arresting both of you for obstruction…or something," Ramsey growled.

Nick sighed as Liza tried to get away. The policeman hadn't eased any of her fears. "Come on, Liza. It'll be all right."

Once they were all seated, Nick said, "Liza wanted to disappear because she feared the man would find her. I offered to bring her here."

The detective shot him a sarcastic grin. "Mighty big of you."

Nick wanted to punch his lights out, but he controlled his anger. "I knew my housekeeper would enjoy the company and could keep an eye on Liza while

I worked. And we could keep her presence a secret. I don't entertain much.''

"You have a housekeeper?"

"Yes," Nick replied succinctly, glaring at the officer.

"I understand the lady's fears and why you'd help her. What I don't understand is keeping it a secret from us. We're here to help."

Nick looked at Liza and nodded.

He was still holding her hand and felt the tension in her. But she gathered her courage and answered the question.

"The problem with telling you, Detective Ramsey, is that you would inform my family."

The detective's hands jerked and his gaze sharpened. "Why would that be a problem, Ms. Colton?"

Liza looked at Nick again and he nodded in support.

"I—I think— It's possible someone in my family is involved."

"Who?"

Liza didn't respond to the sharp question.

Nick spoke up. "What Ms. Colton is asking you, Detective, is if you'll keep her location a secret from anyone else involved in the case. She wanted you to know she hadn't made the phone call so the investigation wouldn't go off-track."

"And what I want to know is who she suspects of being involved in the kidnapping." The man's features were grim and determined.

Nick looked at Liza again. Only she could answer that question.

She licked her lips.

He squeezed her hand in support, but he didn't attempt to answer for her. It had to come from her.

"Before I tell you," Liza began, hesitancy in her voice, "I must warn you that my reasons won't make much sense to you." She shrugged. "That doesn't stop me from believing them."

"Okay."

"My—my aunt Meredith and my cousin were involved in an accident nine years ago. When I first returned to Uncle Joe's house, I discovered Emily pale and frightened. She told me then what she hadn't told anyone else." She paused, seeming to collect her thoughts. "At the time of the accident, she'd seen two Aunt Merediths."

"Did she suffer a head injury in the crash?" the detective asked.

Liza pulled her hand from Nick's and squeezed her two hands together, staring at them. "She had a concussion, but that's not the point, Detective. The point *is* my cousin has remained convinced that she saw two identical women at the accident."

"That doesn't make sense, Ms. Colton."

"I warned you," she pointed out to the detective. "But there was something else. My aunt's behavior changed radically from that day on. She went from being a warm, loving person to a cold, selfish egotist. Her love of gardening, which had turned the home into a paradise, disappeared overnight. The kind, patient employer became a demanding tyrant. The loving wife disappeared. My uncle's marriage has degenerated into…a legal piece of paper.''

"Did your cousin ever confront her?'' Ramsey asked.

"Detective, my cousin was only eleven. And confused. But she did once tell my uncle that she'd seen two Merediths at the wreck. In front of my aunt, who according to Emily, stared at her with hateful intensity and told her to stop being foolish. Since then, my aunt has watched her with evil intent in her gaze.''

"If the woman didn't do anything for nine years, why did things change?''

"A month ago Emily questioned her mother's identity to one of the longtime employees. Meredith overheard her and threatened Emily.''

"Were there any witnesses?''

"No. She may be an awful person, but she's not stupid.''

"Kidnapping seems a strange response,'' the detective pointed out, his gaze calculating as he stared at Liza.

"Yes, it does,'' Liza said.

Nick noted she was calmer now that she'd explained. He thought Ramsey might even believe her, at least a little.

"You see, Aunt Meredith has had two children since the accident. Kidnapping either of those children would've paid off more handsomely than the kidnapping of an adopted child, one would think.''

"Maybe they were more closely guarded," Ramsey suggested.

"Probably, but Emily's bedroom is on the second floor, only accessible by entering the house. Why would they focus on her? And they had to be able to find her room. It had to be on purpose that they chose Emily, not a random kidnapping of anyone connected to Joe Colton."

Admiration rose in Nick as he realized Liza had applied logic to her cousin's situation, in spite of being emotionally involved. She was an intelligent woman. He could tell she'd impressed the detective, too.

"You have a point there, Ms. Colton." He stood and began pacing the room. Then he stopped to face her. "Now, I'm willing to concede that for the moment we should keep your location a secret. But I've got to notify the FBI that you're safe and not involved in the kidnapping. I'm not sure they'll agree to your stipulation. And I've got to call your uncle."

"I know," she whispered. "But, please—"

"I can stall them for a little while. I'll tell them you called us but didn't give your location."

"Thank you!" she said in relief.

"Detective, how much ransom did they ask for?" Nick asked.

"A million dollars. Small potatoes for Joe Colton."

Liza nodded in agreement. "But I thought the man pursuing me meant she'd escaped," she said. "Do you really think the kidnappers have her?"

"I don't know. Maybe he came after you because

your aunt knows Emily spoke to you about the accident."

"That doesn't make sense. But if that were true, then the woman Emily spoke to at the house would be in danger too."

"Her name?"

"Nora. She worked in the kitchen and was upset that Aunt Meredith had chastised her unfairly."

"Nora who?"

"Nora Hickman."

He looked at Nick. "May I use your phone?"

Nick nodded, and both he and Liza watched the policeman as he called the station and talked to the chief, asking him to check on the status of one Nora Hickman. Then he hung up. "He'll call me back here."

Nick spoke. "I do apologize for misleading you, Detective, but I was concerned for Liza's safety. Have the New York City police gone to her apartment?"

"Yeah. They knocked on the door and got no answer. They didn't have a search warrant, so they didn't take it any further."

"I'm sure Liza will give you permission for them to search the premises, to see if they can find fingerprints."

"Oh, yes. I'll even give you a key, if you want. Or I can call the doorman to tell him to let them in," Liza agreed.

"We can manage, as long as you write out something to go in the file. Uh, was your apartment in good condition when you left it?"

"Yes. I have a service that comes in to clean it when I leave town," she assured him.

"Right. I'll—"

The phone rang. Nick answered it and handed the receiver to the detective when the caller identified himself.

"Yeah? I see. Look, I've got permission to search Ms. Colton's apartment in New York. Can you contact the police there and have them do so? I'll have her permission on paper for the files." He listened, then said, "Yeah. She says she has a service come in and clean, so it should be tidy." More silence. "I'm on my way back now."

Detective Ramsey hung up and looked at the two of them. "Okay, we're having the NYPD check out the apartment. I'm going to contact the FBI and bring them up to date, but I don't think I'll have any difficulty keeping your location from your family."

"Why?" Nick asked, afraid of what was coming.

"Because Nora Hickman was killed in an accident, just before your cousin was kidnapped, Ms. Colton."

Liza's gaze filled with pain before she closed her eyes and slumped back against the sofa.

"It could be coincidence," Nick offered.

"Dr. Hathaway, in my business we don't see much coincidence. If we dig deep enough, there's always a reason, a connection. Ms. Colton has just provided the reason without even knowing it had happened."

The detective got to his feet. "I'm not saying you did the right thing keeping this secret, Ms. Colton, but I do understand why you did." He cleared his throat. "I'm not pressing charges against either one of you. But you keep yourself out of sight. Until we get to the bottom of what's going on here, you need to be careful."

Nick couldn't have put it better. And he was grateful the warning was coming from someone else.

Liza nodded but said nothing.

Nick stood to escort the detective to his front door. After they left Liza in the den, Ramsey muttered, "I'd guess you talked her into coming clean. Thanks."

"As long as you don't reveal her location, I'll be glad I did it. I don't want her hurt, though."

"I can understand that. She's a beautiful woman," Ramsey said with a sly grin. Before Nick could protest, the man stepped out the door. "You have any problems, let me know."

"I will," Nick agreed, but after he closed the door, he muttered, "Maybe."

Liza sat in stunned silence after she was left alone. Nora had been killed in an accident? The woman was in her fifties and had worked for the Coltons for years. As the detective had said, coincidence was too convenient.

She'd come so close to losing her own life too. She shivered and covered her face with her hands. What would she have done without Nick's generosity and support? She wasn't dumb, but she wasn't prepared for running, for fighting a man who had no qualms about killing women.

"Liza, are you all right?" Nick asked, his arms going around her.

She hadn't heard him come in. But though she was startled by his touch, her heart immediately swelled with warmth, with gratitude. Remembering the security she'd felt as she'd slept, she slid her arms around his neck and buried her face against his chest. "Nick, I—I owe you so much."

"Nonsense. Anyone would've done the same."

She lifted her face and looked at him, loving his blue eyes, his strong face, the cleft in his chin. "No, that's not true. Most people don't want to be involved if there's trouble."

He reached out and smoothed back her hair. "You would've managed, even if I hadn't offered, honey. You may look like a waif, but you're a strong woman. I was proud of you today."

His words made her feel strong. Aunt Meredith had said them many times, long ago. But since her loving aunt had disappeared, replaced by a cold stranger, no one had held her, praised her like that.

"Oh, Nick," she said a sigh. Then she did something she'd contemplated, something she'd warned herself against. But she couldn't help it.

She reached up and covered his lips with hers.

Nine

Patsy Portman was comfortable in the phone booth in a seedy neighborhood. She'd spent most of her life in less than elegant surroundings like these.

Meredith Colton was jittery, anxious.

The fact that they both occupied the same body made life difficult. For nine years, she'd portrayed Meredith Colton and reaped the benefits—a wealthy husband, a beautiful mansion, everything she wished for.

Except security.

Patsy's perfect plan had a few leaks....

Finally a rough voice answered the phone.

"Have you found her yet?" Patsy demanded, fury in her voice.

"Hell, woman, I've been looking. I can't help it if that bitch can run and hide like a pro."

"She's only twenty. You're the one who's supposed to be a pro. Did you find Liza?"

After a pause, he said, "Yeah. She don't know nothing."

Her voice hard and unyielding, Patsy yelled, "You're lying!"

"No, I'm not! I didn't talk to her myself, but I hired a friend. He talked to her, but a man showed up and he had to run."

"Have him find her again!"

"He tried! He went to New York, to her apartment. She wasn't there." He gave an evil chuckle. "But he'll find her. Bulldog don't give up."

"You stupid bastard! You'd better be right. I won't tolerate any screw-ups."

"Maybe they'll think it's a hoax, that the two worked together. They'll stop looking for me!"

"Looking for you? Why are they looking for you?"

More silence.

Patsy let out a stream of cussing learned during her shady past. Words Meredith had probably never heard. "Listen, you idiot! Be sure you keep the ransom safe, every penny of it, you hear me? Or yours will be the corpse next to Emily's. I'll call, get the money from you as soon as I can get away safely." She hated leaving it in that idiot's hands any longer than necessary.

She slammed down the receiver and exited the

phone booth. In this part of town, no one looked at her. It wasn't safe to be too nosy here. Even if they traced the call to the phone booth, which was impossible, no one would expect Meredith Colton to even know about this side of town, much less visit it.

The only danger was someone seeing her car before she got to the freeway. She reached the car, got in and eased out of the dark alley. No squealing tires. She didn't want to call attention to herself.

But damn, she wasn't going to lose her wealth, her position, because of a stupid bastard who couldn't follow orders. She'd kill him before she'd let that happen. She was so close to having it all.

Someone else was trying to save her the trouble of killing Joe. Then the money would really be hers. All of it.

She was so close.

And no one—not even Emily and Liza—was going to stop her.

Tuesday, Nick pulled into the driveway at what was now his normal time. Before Liza, he would linger at the office, tidying up any possible loose ends. Now he left those details to his staff.

Not that he was being careless. His staff was quite capable. He just hadn't had any personal demands that needed his attention.

Until Liza.

The eagerness he felt as he strode into the house alarmed him a little, but it didn't slow him down. "Hello, I'm home," he called.

Instead of Liza's beautiful voice, Bonnie greeted him from the kitchen.

"Where's Liza?" he demanded, his gaze circling the room.

"My day was fine, thank you," Bonnie replied.

It took a second for Nick to understand her sarcasm. "Oh, uh, yeah, Bonnie, how was your day? And where's Liza?"

The housekeeper chuckled, seemingly okay with his preoccupation with their houseguest.

"She's resting."

Nick frowned. "This late? Is she okay?"

"She may have overdone it a little."

"Doing what?"

"Raking leaves."

Nick's heart sped up. "Out front? You let her rake leaves in the front yard? Did anyone see her?"

"No, of course not. But she pleaded for something to do. So I let her rake leaves in the back. For such a little thing, she's a hard worker."

Nick knew Bonnie was comparing Liza with Daphne, who only would lift a hand to ring for Bonnie. She'd certainly never done yardwork. "She's tall."

Bonnie gave him a disgusted look. "Is that all you can say? Oh, and Nick, when I took her some iced tea to drink, she was singing!"

"Singing? She's not supposed to be using her voice!"

"No, not *singing,* just singing, you know, humming while she worked, occasionally singing words, but just…enjoying herself. It was magical.''

Nick knew her voice was recovering as her body was getting rest and being properly fed. And the tension was lessening. It had increased Sunday, when Detective Ramsey had visited, but yesterday and today, there'd been no incidents or occurrences to remind her that she might be in trouble.

"So she's in her room?''

"Yes. And dinner's almost ready. You want to go get her?''

Oh, yeah! But he immediately dismissed that suggestion. It wasn't safe. When she'd thrown her arms around his neck and kissed him two days ago, he'd almost lost control. He'd almost broken his promise.

"No. Tell me what to do and I'll finish up here while you check on her. It might embarrass her if I wake her up.''

Like it had embarrassed her when he'd pulled her arms from around his neck Sunday night. She'd thought he didn't want her to kiss him. What an innocent!

Last night, the first time they'd had any significant time alone after her kiss, she'd tried to avoid him. While her actions had hurt, he figured they'd been wise, so he hadn't said anything.

Instead he'd listed all the reasons any future didn't exist for the two of them.

Bonnie came down a few minutes later with Liza trailing her. Nick had already carried the baked chicken breasts, green beans and mashed potatoes to the table. Now he was waiting for the rolls to brown.

"Good evening, Liza. How are you?"

"Fine, thank you, Doctor," she said, but she didn't look at him.

"I hear you worked hard this afternoon."

That got her attention. She looked first at Bonnie, then at Nick. "Not really. I raked leaves for a while. I used to do a lot of gardening at Aunt Meredith's when I was young."

"It was kind of chilly out. I wouldn't want you to catch a cold." His gaze remained fixed on her beautiful features, studying her.

"I didn't."

After remaining silent, Bonnie asked, "Are the rolls done yet, Nick?"

He'd completely forgotten about the rolls since Liza came into the room. He hurriedly opened the oven door and snatched the bread pan out of the oven. The rolls weren't burned exactly, just a dark tan.

Avoiding the ladies' gazes, he muttered, "Right on time."

"If you like them crusty," Bonnie said with a grin.

Once they all sat down at the table, he said, "Bonnie mentioned you were singing today."

"Oh, lovey, I didn't mean to get you in trouble," Bonnie said at once, "but it was such a lovely sound, I had to tell Nick."

"Neither one of you is in trouble," Nick growled, irritated that his housekeeper was treating him like

Liza's father. "I just wanted to know how singing made her throat feel."

"I didn't strain my throat. I kept it light, but it felt so good to finally be able to sound normal. I felt... blessed. Thank you for helping me get my voice back."

For the first time since Sunday, she gave him that brilliant smile of hers, one that could light the world. He figured that smile had as much to do with her sell-out concerts as her voice.

"After dinner would you sing something for me?" he asked. "I want to see if I hear any strain."

"Of course," she replied and he was relieved to see eagerness in her eyes.

During the rest of the meal he didn't question her again. She and his housekeeper chatted easily about the day's events. It was easy to see that the two ladies had an excellent rapport.

After they finished eating, Bonnie begged him not to let Liza sing until she'd cleaned the kitchen. Liza's response was to immediately assist in the cleanup, in spite of Bonnie's concern that she might be tired.

"Really, Bonnie, I only raked some leaves. It felt good to move around," Liza insisted.

Nick pitched in, too, and in no time the kitchen was spotless. Then he led the way into the living room where a piano his mother had occasionally played stood against one wall.

"I don't play well but...do you need some accompaniment?" he asked.

"I'll do it," she replied, no sign of nervousness in her.

"You play?"

"Oh, yes. I started with piano lessons, then added the violin and guitar. I'm not an expert at any of them, but I can get by."

She settled on the bench seat and struck a few keys before she looked at him over her shoulder. "What do you want to hear?"

He had no idea what to request. He looked at his housekeeper.

"What you were singing today, lovey? It's one of my favorites."

Liza's green eyes sparkled as she turned around, a smile on her face. Nick thought she'd never looked more beautiful.

"The hills are alive, with the sound of music..." she began in an incredible voice.

Nick was astounded. He'd heard good singers before, but she was more than good. Her voice was liquid silver, shimmering in the air, a sparkling melody that lifted his soul. Right here in his own living room.

The thought that this voice might've been lost to the world sent both fear and thanksgiving through him.

When she finished, he stared at her, unable to speak.

She waited, but he continued to stare.

"That bad?" she asked with a laugh.

Her question spurred him to respond. "That was

incredible, Liza. I'd heard you were good, but you have the most fabulous voice.''

"Oh, yes, lovey," Mrs. Bonnie added. "You're better than Julie Andrews."

Liza chuckled. "I don't think Miss Andrews is losing any sleep over me, Bonnie, but thank you. That's a lovely compliment."

Nick had told himself that he'd never have a future with Liza Colton. He was too old. He wanted a home, a family, neither of which her demanding travel schedule as an entertainer would allow. But deep inside him, he'd still hoped, because the attraction he felt was so strong.

But Liza Colton, the fabulous singer Liza Colton, had just killed that persistent flicker of hope.

Her gift, her voice, was more powerful than his hopes and dreams. How could he deny the world the opportunity to hear her voice?

Even to him that thought seemed melodramatic, but he couldn't deny how moving her voice was. How much it separated their worlds.

He stood. "Well, continue to rest your voice as much as possible, Liza. You're almost well, but we don't want to rush it. Now, if you ladies will excuse me, I have some work to do."

And he left the room.

Both women stared after Nick's departing figure.

"Did I say something wrong?" Liza whispered, speaking to herself as much as Bonnie.

"No, lovey, you didn't. He's probably a little over-whelmed by your lovely voice. It truly is a gift."

Liza blinked several times. "It can be a curse, as well."

Bonnie looked surprised. "Whatever do you mean? Your voice is so special. Everyone must love you!"

"That's not love, Bonnie. They admire my voice. Or they want to profit from my voice. They want the fame my voice can bring, or the money it can earn. But love?" She tried to laugh but the sound was more like a sob. "Love isn't a part of the package."

Bonnie got up and came to the piano to hug Liza. "Lovey, there's more to you than your voice. You're a sweet person, giving and filled with the wonder of life. I can't imagine what monsters would covet your gift but not love you."

Liza rested in the older woman's arms, thinking how seldom she'd received such affection since her Aunt Meredith had changed. With a sniff and another attempt at laughter, she said, "You haven't met my mother."

The next day was Wednesday, the day Emily had promised to call. Liza was nervous all day, though the call was supposed to come between four and five. She helped Bonnie with household chores to pass the time, but she had so many things to worry about, it didn't offer much escape.

In addition to Emily's safety, she wondered where the man who'd come to the hospital had gone. She wondered if the New York City police had found anything at her apartment. The current Meredith worried her too. What would she try next?

And there was the attempt on Uncle Joe's life. She'd been at his sixtieth birthday party when someone had tried to shoot him. That was just before her tour started. She'd considered canceling but her mother had insisted she go. The shooting alone had been shocking, but then Emily had disappeared. Within no time her life had been thrown into turmoil.

And she wondered why Nick had reacted to her singing as he had. Most people, whether she knew them or not, were pleased with her singing. Not Nick.

He'd avoided her the rest of the evening, only saying good-night when she'd gone to his study to tell him she was going to bed. He hadn't even looked at her.

She'd experienced coldhearted withdrawal before, from her parents, from the new Meredith, but she'd never thought Nick would behave in the same manner. After all he'd protected her, nurtured her, been there for her.

No more.

Nick's withdrawal was like a raw, gaping wound. She assured herself she would survive, but it would take time. Which was ridiculous. She'd only known the man for six days.

She sighed. It wasn't logical, the attraction she felt, but she couldn't deny it either.

"Lovey, you need to sit down and have a snack. I promised Nick I wouldn't let you overdo today."

"I haven't, Bonnie, and I have to keep busy or I'll

go crazy." Bonnie stared at her and Liza added, "I'm expecting a phone call from...a friend. I'm anxious to hear from her."

"You haven't gotten any calls so far today. If you had, I would remember, because I'd worry if I should tell you. Nick is so secretive about what's going on. He never even explained about the policeman's visit on Sunday."

Liza gasped. "I didn't think you knew."

"When I heard the doorbell, I looked out my window," Bonnie said. "Those cars the non-uniformed police drive are pretty easy to pick out. You know, plain gray, no markings, like the government cars." She opened the refrigerator and took out some fruit juice for Liza. "I asked Nick about it, but he said it was better if I didn't know."

Liza thanked her for the juice and took a sip, trying to decide what she should say. "Uh, he's probably right."

"So I'm losing sleep? For my own sake?"

"Oh, Bonnie, I'm sorry, but it has nothing to do with you. I'm afraid I've brought all this trouble on Nick. I probably should go." Especially since he didn't want her around any longer.

"I think Nick would be really upset if you left." Bonnie put a motherly arm around her shoulders. "Are you in trouble?"

"Not exactly, but, well, some things have happened, and a man came after me. Nick is helping me hide until he's caught."

"You mean a stalker?" Bonnie exclaimed, her

eyes lit with excitement. "I've read about celebrities having these crazies come after them. Don't you worry, lovey, we'll keep you safe."

Liza smiled her gratitude, but she didn't say anything to correct Bonnie's interpretation. She didn't need to know the threatening soap opera her family seemed to be involved in.

The phone rang and Liza jumped up and raced to it, then realized it wasn't her right to answer. She took a step back and looked at Bonnie.

"Go ahead and answer. If it's not your friend, just take a message."

Liza grabbed the phone, her heart thumping, only to hear a strange woman's voice, asking for Mrs. Allen. "One moment, please."

The housekeeper took the phone and answered her friend's first question. "Oh, she's kind of like a niece, come to visit." Then she chatted for a few minutes before hanging up.

"That was Marie. She works for another doctor. We meet for lunch every week. She said to bring you along," Bonnie said, a question in her gaze.

"I'm sorry, I wish I could. But it wouldn't be smart on my part to advertise my presence."

"No, of course not. I'll tell her you're too young to lunch with a couple of old ladies. We can say you've gone shopping."

Liza agreed, and she knew some young people might feel that way, but she would've enjoyed going out with Bonnie. It would almost be like having Aunt Meredith around again, the good Aunt Meredith.

The sound of a car in the drive caught both ladies's attention. Bonnie hurried to the window. "My goodness, it's Nick home even earlier than yesterday. I'm glad he's not working so hard, but I wonder what's going on."

Liza wondered the same thing. As little interest as he'd shown the past couple of days, she didn't think his early arrival had anything to do with her.

He strode into the kitchen, a frown on his face. "Has she called yet?"

The flood of emotion that filled Liza almost brought her to tears. He hadn't forgotten.

She shook her head. "No, I've been waiting all day."

"I figured you had. I came as soon as my last patient left."

"Thank you, Nick. I—"

The phone rang again. This time Nick answered. "Oh, hello, Detective Ramsey." He looked at Liza as he responded so she'd know it wasn't Emily.

But she didn't lose interest. Detective Ramsey would only call about her or her family.

"Yes, I see. Good, thank you... Yes, I will." Nick hung up the phone and turned around.

"That was Ramsey. As we suspected, your apartment was broken into and ransacked. Did you have anything of value there?"

"You mean money or jewelry? No. I travel so much, I keep those kinds of thing in a safety-deposit box. Did—did he trash it?" The apartment had never really felt like home, but she'd liked it.

"Apparently he did some damage. Your doorman said he would call the service you use to come clean it up. He must've worn gloves because the police didn't get any fingerprints. But the doorman recognized the sketch, said the man was delivering something."

Liza sighed. "I wish they'd catch him, so I could go back to my own life." Even as she said those words, she knew she'd miss Bonnie...and the good doctor.

The phone rang for a third time, and Liza closed her eyes, sending up a silent prayer that this time the caller would be Emily.

She held her breath as Nick reached for the receiver again.

"Hello?"

Ten

Emily Blair Colton hesitated before speaking. "Is— is Liza there?"

The deep voice of the man who'd answered didn't hesitate. "One moment."

Then, blessedly, she heard Liza's voice.

"Liza," she gasped, trying to control the tears that filled her eyes upon hearing her beloved cousin's voice. "Are you all right?"

"Me? You're the one we're all worried about. Tell me what's going on? Did you get the money?"

"Oh, yes, thank you, it's more than enough. I've gotten a job, too, so I won't need any more."

"If you do need more, you know I'll send some," Liza urged.

"I know. But you haven't said if you're all right. Have you seen that man?"

"No, but he broke into my apartment. And he called home asking for me, so I had to talk to the police again."

"Why is— Do you think he's trying to kill you?"

"No, I think he's still looking for you."

"But they have the ransom now. Don't you think they'd stop?" She didn't think so, but that fantasy helped her get through some long nights.

"I hope that's true," Liza said doubtfully. "At least you know Uncle Joe won't regret the money, as long as you're okay."

"I know. Have they found out anything about who tried to kill him? Do they think the two events are connected? I've thought and thought, but why would that woman want to kill Joe? He's her husband!"

"I don't know what's going on. Besides, I haven't understood anything about Aunt Meredith in years." Liza sighed. "What kind of job did you get?"

"I'm a waitress and sometimes cook at a diner. Mom's cooking lessons are paying off. The real Mom." The woman claiming to be Meredith ran from the kitchen.

"But, Emily—" Liza began to protest.

"It's okay, Liza, truly. And I'm becoming friends with Annie Summers. She's a single mom who runs an antique store here in town." Then with a small chuckle, she added, "I've even got a suitor."

"A suitor? What are you talking about, Em?"

"The deputy sheriff. He comes to the diner every

day for lunch. He's shy, but I figured he'd be a good man to know in case—in case I have trouble.''

''Have you told him anything?''

''No, nothing.''

''That's probably wise. I wish I knew more to tell you. But I've been thinking, you should call Rand.''

Emily gasped. ''I can't do that!''

''Why not? He's not at home. You know he's in Washington D.C. He'd probably be able to help you since he's a lawyer.''

''Liza, he's also Meredith's own son. He'd never believe me.''

''You know none of her children are close to her anymore. I think he'd be glad to hear from you.''

''But he'd feel compelled to tell Uncle Joe, for sure. And he might feel he had to tell the FBI. If he didn't, he might be in big trouble. I don't want to cause Rand any problems.'' In spite of Meredith's behavior the past nine years, her children had treated Emily like a true sister. The last thing she wanted to do was cause them difficulties or put a rift between them.

''Oh, Em, you can't hide out forever. I'm worried about you.''

''Oh!'' Emily gasped.

''Em? What's wrong? Is someone scaring you?'' Liza immediately responded.

''No! No, I'm fine, but, Liza, it's snowing!'' The beauty of the scene, compared to the sordidness of her life right now, seemed miraculous. ''It's beautiful.''

"Good heavens, you gave me a heart attack."

"Sorry," Emily said softly. "I guess I'd better go."

"Wait! When will you call again? Can I call you? I might hear something or—or need to talk to you."

"I don't think that would be safe for either of us, Liza. I'll call when I can."

"How about calling Saturday?"

"I work until late Saturday evening. I could call Sunday morning. I'm off then."

"Okay, call me Sunday. But call me sooner if you need help. And think about talking to Rand."

"I will. And you keep safe."

"You, too."

Reluctantly, Emily hung up the phone. She wished she could see Liza, hug her, feel the love they shared. She felt so alone. But Annie's friendship was helping. Only, she had to be careful. Annie was becoming curious about her knowledge of antiques.

And Toby, she really had to keep him at a distance. Which wasn't too bad. He might have a crush on her, but she felt about him the way she did Rand and her other brothers.

She sighed and opened the door to the phone booth, turning up the collar on the cheap jacket she'd bought at an army surplus store. A snowflake drifted down to land on her nose and, in spite of her difficulties, she couldn't hold back a smile.

Liza hung up the phone but remained facing the wall, her eyes closed, trying to hang on to the connection she felt with Emily.

"Who is Rand?" a harsh voice demanded.

She spun around to stare at Nick. "Rand? He's one of my cousins, Joe's oldest son. Why?"

"I heard you mention his name. I wasn't eavesdropping." He tried to excuse his question, but she raised her hand to stop him.

"It's okay. I've brought all this trouble to you, so I think you have the right to know." She paused and then added, "He's a high-powered attorney in Washington D.C. I thought maybe he could help Emily. I don't like the idea of her being a sitting duck for that disgusting man."

"You could bring her here."

Liza shook her head even as her heart swelled at his offer. "I already asked her the first time she called, remember? If you didn't want both of us, I was going to find another place. But she refused, said she felt safe where she was."

"She got the money?"

"Yes, thank you. But she won't take any more." She couldn't prevent a sob. "She's working at a diner."

"Mercy, this is better than a soap opera," Bonnie exclaimed, her gaze wide with interest.

Liza had forgotten the housekeeper was there. Her concentration had first been on Emily, then Nick. "Oh! Mrs. Allen—"

"Bonnie, anything you've heard has to be forgotten," Nick said sternly.

Bonnie slapped her hands on her ample hips and glared at Nick. "You know I wouldn't repeat anything that would harm Liza, Nick Hathaway!"

Liza ran around the kitchen counter to hug the offended woman. "Of course he does. We both do. It's just that we're a little on edge."

"It's okay, lovey, I understand."

Nick cleared his throat. "Well, is supper ready?"

Bonnie glared at her employer, as if he'd questioned her skills as well as her discretion. "It will be in half an hour. Why don't you take Liza to the den so you can finish your *private* conversation. By the time you're finished, I'll have it on the table."

Liza wasn't sure they had anything else to discuss, and she was even less sure that Nick wanted to be alone with her for any reason. But he motioned for her to follow him.

Once they were in the den, he closed the door behind them. "Bonnie will keep quiet. I'd forgotten she was there, so I spoke without thinking."

"I know, me too. I was so relieved to hear Emily's voice that I forgot everything else. How does she cope? To know that someone is trying to kill her, that—"

"You're in the same situation, Liza," he reminded her.

"I know, but I'm not alone. I have you and Bonnie. I can't thank you enough for protecting me. But Emily has no one."

"Maybe she'll find some new friends."

"She already has, but that worries me, too."

Nick stepped closer, resting his hands on her shoulders. "Is Emily a good judge of character? How well does she know whoever she's found?"

"I don't know much about them. She said one of them is a single mother who runs an antique store. She sounds safe enough. The other is a deputy sheriff who has a crush on her."

Liza wasn't surprised that men would be attracted to Emily. In spite of the nightmare she'd lived for the past nine years, she had an innocence combined with strength that was appealing.

Nick's eyebrows soared. "I guess she's a smart cookie, if she's making friends with the law. That's good."

Without thinking, Liza rested her head on Nick's chest, the beat of his heart a reassuring sound. "I hope so," she whispered.

He wrapped his arms around her and rested his cheek on top of her head. "When is she going to call next?"

"Not until Sunday." Her mind still on Emily and her problems, Liza drew from Nick's strength...until her response to the man intruded on her concern for Emily. She tried to push him away, but Nick held her against him.

"I'll—I'll need to stay until Sunday, for Emily's call, but then I probably should leave. I've imposed on you long enough."

"No!" Nick snapped and pressed her closer to him. "It's not safe."

"But lately, I've thought you might be tired of all

the problems I've brought you." She held her breath, waiting for his response.

"No, it's not a problem."

She couldn't stop there. If she was going to stay longer, she had to know what was going on in Nick's head. "Something's wrong. You've changed, Nick, withdrawn. I don't want to stay where I'm not wanted."

Nick couldn't believe she was pinning him in a corner. He had to be honest with her or she'd leave. And if she left, he'd go crazy worrying about her.

He backed off from her and grabbed her arms. "Damn it, Liza! How can you be so unaware?"

She stared up at him with those amazing green eyes. "What are you talking about?"

A sense of calm settled over Nick. It would be a relief to tell her why he'd been holding her at arm's length. Which was a ridiculous thought while he was holding her in his arms. "I'm talking about sexual attraction."

She stared at him blankly and he groaned. "Liza, I want you. I know I'm too old and I know we have no future. I've told myself that over and over again. But I can't keep my hands off you."

"You want me?"

Giving up on words, Nick pulled her tightly against him again and covered her lips with his in a searing, desperate kiss. It had been days since she'd kissed him, and he'd hungered for a repeat every minute of the day and night since then. But it was even better than he remembered.

Her arms reached around his neck, as they had before, and she opened her mouth to him, inviting, encouraging. His tongue teased and tempted, only to have her respond in kind, luring him closer still. Their hearts raced in rhythm and he felt as if his would explode.

He'd been divorced for four years, but he hadn't experienced such incredible attraction or hunger even longer than that. Even when he'd first met Daphne, the world hadn't disappeared the way it did with Liza in his arms.

When he finally had to take a breath, he broke off the kiss and murmured her name, afraid she'd move away, tell him she wasn't interested. Instead, she immediately trailed kisses along his jaw until she reached his mouth again. Those soft, tempting lips were more than he could resist.

He slanted his mouth over hers and lifted her body against him. She was wearing jeans and he slid one hand beneath her rounded, sexy hips to hold her to him, to give her balance, to ensure he could touch as much of her as possible.

Her response had him forgetting time, forgetting all their problems, their differences. All he could think about was Liza.

A rap on the door warned them of Bonnie's presence, but she didn't give them much time since she opened the door immediately afterward.

"Dinner's rea— Oh!" she said as she started backing out the door. "Whenever you're ready," she hurriedly added, a big smile on her face as she closed the door again.

Liza buried her face against his chest.

"Sorry," he whispered. "I got carried away. But at least you understand the problem. I want you to stay here, safe, but if you get too close, I can't promise that won't happen again."

Well, he'd been honest and now he hoped she'd forgive him. She raised her gaze to his face. He studied her, but he didn't see horror, anger, repulsion, or any of the emotions he'd feared. But he couldn't read anything in that stare.

Maybe she was in shock.

He certainly was. He'd wanted her. That didn't take a rocket scientist to figure out. But he hadn't known how badly he wanted her, how desperately he wanted more of her. How even more difficult it was going to be to keep his distance in the future.

Realizing he was still holding her against him, he forced his arms to release her. "Uh, I'd—I'd better go wash up for dinner." And get his body under control. It seemed determined to ignore his admonition for caution. And it definitely wanted to ignore his order to let her go.

In fact, he wasn't sure he was going to be able to let her go. But she helped him, taking a step back, still staring at him. His arms fell uselessly to his sides, as if they had no reason to exist if they weren't holding Liza.

Her gaze was fixed on his lips, and he wanted to

taste her again, but some noise in the background forced him to come to his senses. Was Bonnie listening outside the door? That thought had him stepping away from her even farther. How embarrassing to lose control at his age.

Even worse to play the classic role of a man in a midlife crisis losing his mind over a gorgeous Lolita. Not that he was that old, or that Liza had in any way plotted to seduce him. He wished. But he was definitely losing his mind.

"I have to go."

Then he bolted from the room.

Liza stared at the door.

She'd just spent the most ecstatic, devastating, memorable moments in Nick's arms that she'd ever experienced. She'd thought she was in love with the man her mother had paid off. She'd been sure she was heartbroken when he walked away with the money—and without her.

But she'd been wrong. Not until this moment had she experienced anything earth-shattering. Nick Hathaway had taken her heart for his own.

She suspected she'd never be able to claim that part of her body again.

So what was she going to do?

He'd said they had no future. He'd made it clear he only wanted sex. Tears pooled in her eyes, because she wanted so much more. But what did she have to offer? All she brought with her was trouble. When everything was settled, would he still want her?

Could she wait until her difficulties were resolved to tell him how much she wanted from him?

That she might be able to do, but she wouldn't be able to resist his arms, his lips, all of him, not even for a New York minute. She wanted him, however she could get him.

She walked out of the den, her head high. She wasn't going to be ashamed that she was attracted to the man, or apologize for responding to him. She'd have to be dead for that not to happen.

When she entered the kitchen, Bonnie immediately asked her to pour the drinks for their dinner, making it easy to pretend she hadn't interrupted a torrid love scene.

When Nick finally came down, dinner was on the table and she and Bonnie were talking about a weather report the housekeeper had heard.

"Did you know that, Nick?"

"What?" he asked, his voice clipped.

"Bonnie says it may snow tonight. The temperature is supposed to drop to near freezing," Liza said, smiling at him.

He seemed surprised by her composure. She raised her chin a notch. He might think he was too old for her, but she sure wasn't too young for him.

"No, I hadn't heard that. It's a little early for our first snow."

Bonnie chipped in. "It probably won't snow, but at least everyone will get excited anticipating it."

A quick glance at Nick told Liza he recognized how those words could apply to what happened in the den. At least he was as aware of her as she was of him.

"Emily— I mean my friend said it had started snowing there."

"Where?" Bonnie asked.

It occurred to Liza that she'd better think about what she was saying. She didn't intend to reveal Emily's location, even if Bonnie didn't know her story. "Out west," she said casually.

Bonnie pretended her response was normal. "I guess they get a lot of snow out there."

"Yes. Are we ready to eat?"

"A'course. Everyone sit down. It's your favorite tonight, Nick. My famous meat loaf."

There was little conversation at the table. When Bonnie made a comment on the weather, or her day, either Nick or Liza would respond briefly and the topic would be abandoned.

Liza was busy debating what she should do. Obviously she and Nick couldn't co-exist with the tension as high as it was. *Could* she leave? Should she leave?

"More rolls, Liza?"

"What? Oh, no, thank you, Bonnie. But they're delicious."

"Homemade," the woman responded proudly.

Liza nodded.

"Bonnie is famous for her rolls," Nick added, his gaze flickering to Liza before he looked back down at his plate.

Scintillating conversation.

* * *

Nick's stomach was churning. He'd barely eaten anything of his favorite meal. Stirring his food, he'd managed a bite here or there, but his plate still held a lot when he shoved back from the table.

Bonnie stared at his plate and then at him, but much to Nick's relief, she didn't comment on his lack of appetite.

"There's a wonderful program on PBS this evening on that famous train ride across Canada. Anyone want to watch it with me?" she said instead.

Nick held his breath, waiting for Liza's response.

"Oh, yes, I'd love to see that," she replied, smiling at his housekeeper.

He coveted that smile. But she hadn't even looked directly at him since— No, he wouldn't think about when he'd held her in his arms. He nodded his head. "That sounds good, Bonnie. Maybe we could even share some popcorn."

"Why, of course, Nick. That's a good idea. You two go on in and I'll—"

"No!" he and Liza replied at once.

Liza added, "I'll fix some drinks, Bonnie. I'll need one to counteract the saltiness."

"I'll go turn on the television," Nick said. He knew Liza wouldn't come into the room without Bonnie. A good thing, since he doubted he could trust himself to be alone with her.

He still felt the same way when he climbed the stairs to his bedroom several hours later. He'd waited until the ladies had retired, then he'd made sure the house was locked up.

Returning to his home office, he'd picked up the murder mystery he'd been wanting to read. He knew sleep wasn't going to come easily. His mind—and his body—was still focused on Liza.

A few minutes later he settled against the piles of pillows and picked up the book. The cover didn't faze him, a dagger with drops of blood. He was thinking about Liza.

"Get a grip, man," he muttered.

Then he heard a knock on his door.

His heart began thumping rapidly even though he told himself it was probably Bonnie. He wasn't sure Liza even knew where his bedroom was. He slipped on his robe and crossed the room.

Wrong move, he deduced moments later when he swung open the door to discover Liza. She was dressed in one of the negligees he'd bought her, and smiling at him.

Eleven

"**W**hat's wrong?"

Liza stared at him. For a man who had professed to want her only a few hours earlier, he seemed remarkable obtuse.

"Nothing's wrong," she said calmly, noting his bare chest beneath the robe. She stepped over the threshold, closing the door behind her.

He backed away from her. "Liza, you shouldn't be here."

Well, this was awkward! She'd assumed he'd realize what she wanted when he saw her. Did she have to spell it out?

Apparently so.

"Nick, I've been doing a lot of thinking about— about this afternoon."

"You should get a glass of milk. That will help you sleep."

She glared at him. "Sleep won't take care of my problem."

"You're sick? Tell me what's wrong."

She was so irritated, she considered heading back to her bedroom. But she loved this hardheaded man. She might not have a future with him, but she would have memories…if he'd cooperate. Instead of speaking, she untied the silken cord of her robe and let the long-sleeved garment fall to the floor, leaving her in a slip of a sheer nightgown.

Nick took another step back and swallowed. Then, his voice hoarse, he said, "Liza, I warned you I don't have as much control as I thought. You need to go to your room and I'll call Bonnie to—"

"I don't want Bonnie," she assured him, her chin rising. "I want you."

"No, you— What did you say?"

"Do I have to beg?"

"You want me? You mean—"

"I should've worn one of those advertising sandwich boards with my message spelled out in bright red letters. Then maybe you'd finally catch on."

"Honey, I told you there's no— We can't— Damn!"

Much to her relief, he stopped talking and took her into his arms. She pressed against him, her arms sliding inside his robe, up his bare chest. She loved the feel of him.

"Are you sure?"

She liked their way of communicating without words. She kissed him.

He got the message.

In seconds, he'd swept her into his arms and carried her to his bed, laid her down and stretched out beside her. His kiss was deep, long-lasting, hot, demanding, all the things she liked. She tried to match his ardor.

"Your robe," she complained when she came up for air. She'd pushed it back from his chest, but she wanted it out of the way.

"Liza, I sleep in the nude," he whispered, his cheeks turning red.

Her gaze lit up. Perfect. She reached for his belt. Before she could undo it, he said, "I think you should join me."

At least he wasn't resisting anymore. She gladly slipped from her gown, but her gaze remained fixed on him, watching him rid himself of his robe.

Then they came together so quickly, so wildly, she knew he'd been honest when he said he wanted her. Her heart sang as she explored his body while he explored hers.

Just when she was sure she could wait no longer for the ultimate togetherness, he pulled back.

"What?" she asked, barely able to speak.

"I'm not prepared!"

Not prepared. "But you said you wanted me."

"Damn it, Liza, I don't have any condoms. I haven't— It's been a long time for me."

Liza closed her eyes so he couldn't see the pain

that struck her. But she whispered, "It's okay. I'm protected."

Much to her pleasure, Nick didn't hesitate after that. He fulfilled every fantasy she'd ever had about sharing such intimacies with the one man in the world she loved. The one man she'd always love. If she hadn't been sure of that before, she was sure of it afterward, when they lay beside each other, breathing deeply, still wrapped in the oneness they'd shared.

"Nick," she whispered.

He wrapped his arms around her and kissed her gently.

Then, in a gravelly voice, he said, "Go to sleep, honey."

Much to her surprise, she did.

When the alarm went off the next morning, Nick quickly hit the sleep button, then shut off the alarm. He'd slept better than he had in years, and the temptation to pull Liza close again and go back to sleep was strong.

But if Bonnie didn't hear the shower, she'd be up the stairs to see what was wrong. He figured Liza would be horribly embarrassed if the housekeeper caught her in his bed.

"Do we have to get up?" Liza mumbled.

"Sorry, honey. I do, but you can sleep late." He kissed those soft lips.

She opened those green eyes before closing them again and meeting his kiss more than halfway.

"Liza, I don't have a lot of time," he said as the kiss ended. "Tonight—"

"Then you'd better hurry," she said before kissing him again.

With that offer, he didn't hesitate, especially since holding her had him already aroused.

Afterward he left her in his bed, dozing off, and ran for the shower. It was hard to leave after he'd dressed, though. Just seeing her in his bed brought a big smile to his face.

When he heard Bonnie coming up the stairs, he had no choice. He reached the top of the stairs the same time she did.

"I was wondering where you were. Your eggs are getting cold," she warned.

"No problem." He thought about warning Bonnie not to bother with his room today, but he knew it would make her curious. He decided to leave well enough alone and hope Liza woke up before Bonnie started her upstairs cleaning.

Liza felt calmer, safe, wanted, more than she ever had. She'd spent the day helping Bonnie with her cleaning, then retreating to the living room where the piano was.

When she'd been younger, before she'd made her first record and begun touring, she'd written songs. In the past few years, though, the music had disappeared. But today it bubbled up in her, trying to break out.

Curious, and pleased, she wanted to explore what

was happening. She played with the tunes that were whirling in her brain, adding words that spoke of love, with Nick's image in her head.

She was still at it when she heard Nick's voice. She sprang up from the piano bench and headed for the back door, throwing herself into his arms when she reached him.

Nick held her close, and the fear she'd hidden all day that he might not want her again was wiped away.

"I missed you," he whispered.

"I was afraid you'd be tired of me," she returned, her lips touching his neck.

Laughter rumbled through him. "You're crazy."

"Yes. Oh, Nick, come let me show you," she pleaded, excitement in her voice as she took his hand and tugged him toward the living room.

She sat down at the piano and played and sang her new song, as proud as a newborn baby's mother. "Do you like it?"

"I love it, but I've never heard it before. Have you recorded it?"

"Oh, Nick, you don't understand. I wrote it today."

He appeared stunned. "In one day?"

"Sometimes that's the way it happens. When I'm very happy, or sometimes when I'm very sad, I hear melodies in my head."

He pulled her up from the piano bench. "Can I assume it's happiness that inspired you today?" he whispered, wrapping his arms around her.

"Oh, yes," she returned and lifted her lips to his.

When he broke off the kiss, he whispered, "Let's go upstairs."

"Won't Bonnie think—"

"I'll take care of Bonnie. Go on up. I'll be right there."

Liza was thrilled that he would want her so soon. With a quick kiss on his lips, she beamed at him and raced up the stairs. All day she'd thought of him. Had she finally found the one person in the world to love? A man who would love her in return?

He'd said they had no future, but he'd loved her like they had one. Maybe, with time, he'd realize how perfect they were together.

Nick strolled into the kitchen. He liked Bonnie, maybe even loved her like a mother, but he wasn't going to let her control his behavior.

"Evening, Nick. You're home a little early. When do you want dinner?" she asked, scarcely looking up from whatever she was doing.

"Not for a while. Bonnie, Liza and I are going upstairs for a while. We'll come down when we're ready." In other words, don't bother us. He hoped she got the message.

With a big smile, she nodded. "No problem."

"You're not going to object?"

"If you're both happy, I am. And it's about time, I think." She looked up at him. "Tomorrow, shall I move her clothes to your room?"

Well, that was certainly cutting to the chase. But

he didn't even have to think about his answer. "Yeah, that'll be great, if it's what Liza wants."

Then he hurried upstairs.

Friday night, Bonnie went to the movies with her friend.

For the first time, Nick and Liza had the house to themselves. Even though Bonnie had tried not to get in their way, they'd also tried to be circumspect, not going to bed until a proper hour.

Tonight, Nick allowed Liza to eat, but then he took her hand and pulled her upstairs.

"But, Nick," she protested, sounding scandalized, "it's only six o'clock."

He pulled her into his arms as they reached the top of the stairs and kissed her. "You don't want me?" he pouted.

"Of course I do, silly," she returned, beaming at him. Her enthusiasm was one of her endearing qualities, among others, that he loved. "But it's still daylight outside."

"It's getting dark. We're approaching winter. You don't mind winter, do you?"

"No, of course not. I like snow."

"Good. And we have short days, which is good if you only want to have sex when it's dark. Winter will become my favorite season."

He grinned when she slapped his shoulder and complained, "Oh, you!"

"Come on, I'm in a hurry!"

Later, they lay in his big bed, wrapped in each other's arms, sated for the moment.

Stroking her soft skin, he murmured, "I think I owe you a big thank-you."

She looked at him with a smile. "Well, I was good, I'll admit, but you were just as good." Her teasing look delayed their conversation because Nick couldn't resist kissing her, several times.

Then he snuggled her up against him. "No, I meant for giving me back my belief in life. I'd dreamed of having a houseful of children and a loving wife, a life like my parents. But after Daphne…well, I wasn't sure I'd ever feel optimistic about anything."

When she didn't move or speak, he looked down at her. "Liza? Are you okay?"

"Yes," she answered, her voice weak. "Are you hungry again? Bonnie bought ice cream today and fixings for sundaes."

"In a little while. Have you thought about having children? I know you're younger than me, but—"

"Quit saying that! You're not old." Then she slid on top of him and encouraged him to prove his strength and virility.

He couldn't refuse that invitation, so their conversation got sidetracked.

But he brought it up again when they were eating the ice-cream sundaes Liza had made an hour later. "You didn't ever answer my question. Have you thought of having children?"

"Yes."

He frowned. There was no enthusiasm in her voice.

He opened his mouth to ask her what was wrong, but she spoke before he could.

"I gather you want children?"

He smiled, staring into the distance. "Oh, yeah. My parents were so looking forward to grandchildren. My sister and one of my brothers both had children before Mom and Dad died. But I'd still like to have kids. To carry on the family, yes, but more than that. I want to teach my son to fish, like my dad taught me. And I'd love a little girl to cuddle, to take to dancing lessons...to walk her down the aisle when I finally have to give her up. But he'd better be good to her!" he added fiercely.

He brought his gaze back to Liza. She wasn't smiling. "Liza?"

"More ice cream?"

Blankly, he looked at his bowl. It was empty. "I don't think so." He stood and carried his bowl to the sink. But he didn't have any intention of ending the discussion. It was too important to him.

Liza stood, too, and took her bowl to the sink, even though it still had a lot of ice cream in it. "I think I'm going upstairs to soak in a hot bath. I'm a little sore." She reached up and kissed him and then walked away before he could pull himself together.

He had been demanding the past two days. When he'd understood how willing she was to be with him, he hadn't held back. He felt guilty that he'd overdone it.

So, he'd give her some space. Maybe they'd watch a movie tonight, a comedy.

Then they'd talk later.

* * *

Liza lay in the hot bath, tears streaming down her face. Had she ever thought of having kids? Oh, yeah. But when she was eighteen and went to the doctor for birth control, he'd told her not to bother. After an examination, he'd told her scars from surgery she'd had when she was a child would make it almost impossible for her to get pregnant.

She'd shed many tears at the time. Then she'd had another doctor examine her, to be sure. He'd given her the same diagnosis.

She'd vaguely held out some hope based on that "almost," but she'd never taken birth control pills, as if daring the fates to give her what she wanted. But she'd remained barren.

She thought she'd accepted her fate. But when Nick began talking about his children, the hurt had been worse than ever. Because it had also meant the end to her hopes of the future. If she couldn't give Nick the children he so badly wanted, then she couldn't marry him.

Nick should have whatever he desired. He was such a good man, tender, kind, loving. He'd be a perfect father, the kind every little boy should have, the kind every little girl dreamed of.

She certainly had.

To have a daddy who cared, who protected, who loved you. Uncle Joe had been good to her, but her own father seldom took any interest in her. Even

Jackson, her brother, hadn't drawn much interest from their father.

When Liza learned that her father had had an affair with Meredith—the new Meredith, his own brother's wife—that had resulted in Meredith's youngest child, Liza had stopped hoping her father would turn to her.

She had no respect for him.

She'd kept his secret, but it was for Uncle Joe's sake. Her father didn't even know she knew. She'd overheard a conversation between Meredith and him. Her mother wasn't the kind of mother little girls needed, but at least she hadn't done something so dishonorable.

But Nick? Nick would be a perfect father.

She couldn't deny him his dreams.

"You knew all along you didn't have a future," she muttered to herself. But that had been before he'd taken her into his arms and made them one. Before he'd given her the wonderful gift of his love. He hadn't said he loved her, but she believed he did.

As she loved him.

But he didn't know her flaws, especially the most important one.

There was a knock on the bathroom door. "Hey, have you drowned? You've been in there long enough to shrivel up."

"It's a new diet theory," she said, trying to keep from revealing the tears in her throat.

"Like you need to diet. I thought we'd watch a movie when you get out. How about *Charade*? It's an oldie but goodie."

"Great. I'll be right out."

She didn't move until she heard his steps moving away from the door. Then she scrubbed her face in the still-warm water, hoping he wouldn't notice her red-rimmed eyes.

When she got down to the den in her nightgown and robe, she found Nick reading a medical journal, a bowl of popcorn and a couple of sodas sitting on the coffee table in front of him.

He looked up at once. "You must be the cleanest human being on earth by now."

"Of course. That's my claim to fame," she assured him, working on her smile.

"Well, come let me get a whiff of you so I can really appreciate all that effort."

She didn't hesitate. After several heated kisses, she was surprised when he released her. "We'll have to start the movie, or we'll be up all night." He leaned forward and picked up the remote.

Liza stared at him. Had he figured out what was wrong with her? Did he not want her anymore? She couldn't complain, in case she was right, so she lay her head on his shoulder and watched the opening credits of the movie he'd chosen.

By the time it ended, she agreed with him. The movie was wonderful. And she would've liked to point out that the hero was older than the heroine. And the heroine had had to work hard to convince him, just as she'd had to convince Nick that she wanted him.

"Did you like it?"

"I loved it," she assured him, smiling but giving no details.

"Good. Ready for bed?"

She nodded. She was ready for him. But after that first night, she'd never had to insist. He'd initiated the lovemaking. So she headed for the bedroom.

They got ready for bed with no conversation. Liza slid under the covers first and waited for her lover. When he turned out the lights and joined her, she scooted closer.

"Night, Liza," he murmured and turned his back to her.

Stunned, she lay there in the dark, then she tapped him on the shoulder. "I think you forgot something," she said stiffly. Okay, she'd accepted the fact that they had no future. At least she was trying. But that didn't mean she was willing to say goodbye tonight.

"What?"

"You didn't kiss me good-night."

"Um, honey, I can't."

That stopped her. Why couldn't he? "You're coming down with a cold?"

"No."

"So you don't want me anymore?"

That had him turning back to face her. He grabbed her hand and let her feel for herself how much he wanted her. Then he groaned.

"But I don't understand. If you want me—"

"You said you were sore!" He huffed a big sigh. "I'm not a monster to insist on making love when it might hurt you, honey. I'm trying to be a gentleman about this.''

"Oh, Nick, I just wanted to soak in a tub. I'm fine. I don't want a gentleman. I want you!''

His arms wrapped around her. "Hey, are you saying I'm not a gentleman?''

She smiled and kissed him. Then she said, "I'm saying you're perfect, and I want you.''

He didn't hesitate then, and they made glorious love. Maybe even more passionately than ever because Liza now knew the time would come when she'd have to leave.

When Nick had fallen asleep, she stared into the dark, silent tears sliding from her eyes onto the pillow.

Paradise, with Nick, wasn't for her.

And she couldn't even explain why. Because he'd deny himself his dream. She already knew that much about him.

So she'd have to be strong and walk away.

But not tonight.

Twelve

Over the next couple of days, as long as Liza could live from day to day, she'd never been happier.

Her days were spent helping Bonnie with the housework and writing music. Her evenings were filled with Nick. Only concern about Emily worried her. She was due to call Sunday morning again, and Liza had a problem.

She needed to prepare for her departure from Nick's house because she didn't know exactly how long she could stay there. She'd even called Detective Ramsey to see if there was any word on the man who'd broken into her apartment. The detective could only tell her they were watching her apartment, but the man hadn't shown up again.

When she had to leave, she didn't know if she'd

be able to go back to her apartment. But she needed a number so Emily would know where to call her.

And she didn't want to have that discussion in front of Nick.

So she'd been devising various ways to take the call from Emily alone, without either Bonnie or Nick hearing her. So far, her plans weren't too impressive.

There was so much she wanted to tell Emily. They'd always shared their deepest hopes and dreams with each other. Emily knew about Liza's physical limitations. She'd want to know if Nick knew, if Liza told her how she felt about him. Liza didn't want to discuss that situation. But she wanted to tell Emily about what she felt in Nick's arms and the joy that filled her...until she remembered that it would soon end.

When the phone finally rang on Sunday morning, about eleven-thirty, she was in the kitchen, helping Bonnie prepare dinner. Bonnie answered the phone and then handed it to Liza. She felt awkward asking to take the call in the den, so she'd just need to be careful of what she said.

"Liza, are you all right?" Emily asked after they'd greeted each other.

"Of course."

"Well, you sound uncomfortable. Is someone with you?"

"Yes." She should've known Emily would understand.

"But you're all right?"

"For the time being, but...things change."

"Are you talking about moving somewhere else? How will I reach you?"

"At home."

"The apartment in New York, or in California?"

"The first," Liza said carefully.

"Would that be safe? What about that horrible man? Won't he find you? Don't go back to your apartment, Liza," Emily urged. "Couldn't you disguise yourself, check into a hotel in New York City with a different name?"

Liza tried to figure how to explain the difficulty to her cousin. "But can't I call you?"

"Oh. You don't know the number to give me, do you? Okay, I'm using another name, Emma Logan. Call the Mi-T-Fine Café in Keyhole." Then she gave her the number, before adding, "Ask for the name I gave you. Then I'll call you later when I'm off work."

"Are you sure you'll be safe?" Liza asked, not wanting her problems to complicate Emily's life. She already had a lot to deal with.

"No, that'll be fine."

"Have you thought about Rand?"

"Yes, but I'm not ready to do that."

"But, Em, I really think—"

"I can't, Liza, I just can't. Any word about Dad? Is he still all right?"

"As far as I know. I haven't heard anything. I haven't even checked my messages because I didn't want to leave this number on the caller ID in the apartment."

"Oh, I hadn't thought of that," Emily said.

"Look, I'll find a way to check before you call next. When will that be?"

"Should I call this number until I hear from you?"

"Yes. Next Wednesday?"

"Okay, but it will have to be about this time. I'm working the late shift all next week."

"Okay. I'll be here, and I'll try to get all the information I can. Take care of yourself, Em."

"You, too, especially if you move. Are you sure you can't stay there?"

"I don't know."

"You're worrying me, Liza. Is the doctor being difficult? I mean, he's not hitting on you, is he?"

Liza almost broke into hysterical laughter. If anything, she was the one hitting on him. But she loved him—which was the reason she couldn't stay. "No, he's fine. How about your deputy?"

"Sweet but shy, so I'm not having any problems. Look, I have to go. I have errands to run before I go to work, but I'll call on Wednesday. Take care of yourself."

"You, too," Liza said, wishing she could see her cousin in person. She hung up the phone, feeling sad and a little frightened. Since Nick had taken her into his home, she hadn't felt like this, but knowing that she would have to leave reminded her that the world was a frightening place.

"You okay?" Bonnie asked.

She turned around to see the housekeeper watching her, concern in her gaze. "Yes, I'm fine."

"I think I have an answer to one of your problems. Not that I was eavesdropping, you know, but you mentioned being unable to call your apartment. You could ask Nick to call and pick up the messages from his offices. It would be normal for your doctor to follow up with a phone call. No one would think anything of him doing that."

Suddenly, Liza was glad she hadn't taken the call in private, because Bonnie's solution to one of her problems was perfect. "That's terrific, Bonnie. I'll ask Nick as soon as he gets home from church."

"I don't think it'll take much persuasion," Bonnie said, grinning. "If you asked him to swim an ocean, I suspect he'd dive in at once."

Liza blinked away the sudden tears. "Oh, I wouldn't make that kind of demand," she said. She wouldn't even insist that Nick marry her when she couldn't give him children. But she would ask about retrieving her phone messages.

Nick, of course, was willing to retrieve her messages. He even suggested they go to his office after their meal. Liza was thrilled at the idea of going out, but she worried about the safety factor.

"Are you sure it'll be safe?"

"On the weekends no one is around, so you can listen to the messages yourself. But just to be safe, you can put on a hat or something."

Liza eagerly leaned forward. "Bonnie, do you have a hat I can borrow?"

"Even better, I have a blond wig you can wear," she said, beaming at Liza. "I wore it for a costume party years ago. Don't know why I kept it, but it's packed away in the attic.''

"Wonderful. I'm excited that I can go out. Not that I don't love it here,'' she hastily added as Nick frowned. "But I might have a little touch of cabin fever.''

"Well, of course you do,'' Bonnie agreed. "I certainly would if I never even got to go to the grocery store, much less the movies or shopping.''

"We're not doing any of those things, Liza. We're only going to the office.''

"I know. But I appreciate it, Nick. I really do.''

An hour later she settled into the front seat of Nick's Mercedes, Bonnie's blond wig securely pinned on. She felt like a little girl playing dress-up, but if it got her safely into Nick's office to collect her messages, it was worth it.

"How is Emily?'' he asked as he drove.

"Oh, fine. She seems comfortable.''

"No problems? Bonnie thought maybe you were upset about something. She said you sounded nervous.''

Liza caught her breath. She didn't want to lie to Nick, but she had no choice. "I'm worried about her. Hiding long-term is different from hiding for a few days. I'm afraid that man will eventually catch up with her.''

"Hmm. Detective Ramsey said the guy who came to the hospital and the apartment hadn't been seen since.''

"Yes. But then he thinks this whole affair is about

money,'' Liza said grimly. A difference of opinion compared to her and Emily's thoughts.

"So you think he's still after Emily even though the money's been collected?''

"Yes.''

Nick frowned but said nothing else as he pulled into the parking lot of his office. He drove to the back of the building, where his private entrance was.

"Wait here until I get the door unlocked, then hurry in, okay?'' He didn't wait for agreement, assuming she would do as he asked.

And she did. He was a little dictatorial, but in this case, he was also right. When he swung the door open, she hurried from the car and the bright sunshine into the shadowy hallway. Then he unlocked his private office.

She sank down into a chair in front of his desk and reached for the phone. He slid a pad and pen across the desk so she could write down any messages she listened to.

With shaky fingers, she dialed her apartment number. It made her nervous to contact the outside world, to step away from Nick's protection. What would it do to her when she had to leave?

The first five calls were from her mother. Her irritated voice demanded that Liza call her, demanded that Liza return to her tour, demanded that Liza obey her mother. Then there was a cautionary call from Uncle Joe, concern in his voice about her safety, about Emily. Her eyes filled with tears and Nick reached out to take her hand.

"You okay?"

She nodded. The next message was from the man who broke into her apartment, threatening her. Her gaze widened in fright. "It's him!"

"Who?" Nick demanded.

"That man! The one who—"

Nick punched a button for the speaker phone.

"I'm gonna find you, bitch, and you'll get what you deserve, you and your little cousin. So say your prayers, because doomsday is coming soon!"

Liza closed her eyes, shuddering.

There were only a couple more calls from her mother. When she hung up, Nick picked up the phone.

"We've got to inform Detective Ramsey about that call."

"But, Nick, it—it makes it clear he doesn't have Emily, and that murder is his intention."

"I know. Ramsey needs to know what's going on, honey. We have to call him."

Liza finally nodded. She wasn't sure how the detective would react, but Nick was right. They had to tell him.

Ramsey wasn't working, but when Nick explained why they'd called, the receptionist offered to call the detective at home and have him call Nick at his office.

Liza stood and crossed to the window, her back to Nick. He hung up the phone and came to her side, putting an arm around her. "Are you all right?"

"Yes, of course. Just worried."

The phone rang.

Nick explained the situation to the detective and he promised to be at the office in ten minutes. Nick directed him to come to the back of the building. He'd be watching for him.

When the detective arrived, Liza replayed her messages, this time on the speaker phone. When he'd heard the message from the man who'd broken in to her apartment, he asked to hear it again.

Then he looked at Liza. "He wants to kill both of you. There's no mention of the ransom."

"You said they already collected the ransom."

"How long have you known that murder was his intention, instead of kidnapping, Ms. Colton, because I don't think you mentioned that before."

The man was frowning at her, and Nick stepped to her side in a protective move that made her feel better. "I actually wasn't sure, but if it was caused by... someone in the family, it didn't make sense. Uncle Joe is generous and has a lot of money."

"I guess I should've picked up on it earlier when the kitchen worker was killed."

Liza stared at him. "Did you get the details of her death?"

"Just that it was hit and run."

Nick asked, "Did they get a description of the car? Who was it registered to?"

"It was stolen, reported only a half hour before the accident, then found abandoned a few miles away. No fingerprints," he added, as if anticipating Nick's next question.

The detective paced the office for several minutes and Liza sat silent, waiting.

Nick had a question, though. "They got no leads when the ransom was paid?"

"No. No leads. The guy escaped clean as a whistle. The feds were so sure they had everything covered." He sounded disgusted. "There's been no contact since. And no sight of your cousin." He rubbed his forehead. "In fact, this," he said gesturing to the tape, "is the first indication that she might still be alive."

"Didn't they mark the money in some way? Has any of it been spent?" Nick asked.

"Yeah," Ramsey said, frowning at them, "it's all marked."

"Won't he know that?" Liza demanded.

The detective shrugged his shoulders. "Depends on how bright he is."

Liza's shoulders slumped and tears gathered in her eyes. She'd really hoped the ransom would provide a lead, so the nightmare could end.

"Can't they question Mrs. Colton?" Nick asked.

"On a bizarre story from her niece?" The detective turned to Liza. "Sorry, ma'am, I don't mean that as an insult. But the FBI doesn't want to turn the Coltons against them. Right now, Mr. Colton is giving his full cooperation, but coming to him with a story like that might change things." He paused and looked again at Liza, his gaze spearing her this time. "Unless you have some proof your aunt was involved?"

She shook her head.

"Yeah, well, too bad that guy didn't incriminate

Mrs. Colton on the answering machine. That would've made a difference."

Nick stood, assuming the interview was over. "Thank you for coming, Detective. We thought you should hear that message."

"You were right. Ms. Colton, do you mind if I copy that message? If you'll give me the number and the code to retrieve messages, I can do that at the office."

Liza couldn't see any harm in that, so she rattled off her phone number and the voice mail code.

The detective departed, presumably for the office, leaving Nick and Liza alone.

Nick came to sit on the arm of her chair, putting his arm around her shoulders. "Sorry, honey. I'd hoped the message would provide the proof that would resolve everything."

"Me, too," she murmured, fighting back tears. "I want this situation to be over. I want Emily to be able to come home…and be safe."

"Yeah…but I don't want you to leave," he whispered before his lips covered hers.

She didn't want to leave either. But she would. And it would have nothing to do with the man on the tape. Only Nick wouldn't know that.

Meredith couldn't escape Joe's, and the FBI's, presence until late that night when she supposedly retired to sleep. At least the idiot had escaped without being captured. That would've ruined all her plans.

She parked near the ratty bar where she'd planned

to meet Silas. It took time for her eyes to adjust to the smoky, gloomy light of the joint, but she discovered Silas exactly where she'd told him to be. The back booth, as far from the light as possible.

She wasted no time with hello. "Where's the money?"

"In the backpack." He slid the heavy pack across the table, staring at the bag like he was afraid it would disappear.

Meredith slid it to the seat beside her, next to the wall. It took her only minutes to determine she'd been set up. "These bills are in consecutive numbers."

"So? They spend as good as any others."

"You idiot! Don't you realize that these bills can't be spent? They'll track us down as soon as they appear." Damn, she'd hoped to at least get some financial relief from the fiasco.

"But I got plans!" Silas protested, his voice rising in distress.

"Keep your voice down, you idiot!" Meredith scolded. "If you ever complete the job, I might pay you," she growled. "When are you going to get rid of her?"

"That bitch hides real well. You got all this money, so you can pay a little more now. Chasing her down is expensive."

"Didn't you hear me? This money is useless. I can give you five thousand, but—" She stopped when he reached for the backpack, as if he intended to take his five grand from the bag. "No, you idiot! We can't spend this money, I'll have to get some different money. Unless you want to go to jail for life.''

He jerked his hands back as if they'd been scalded. ''I got to have more money,'' he whined.

''I'll get it for you, but not this money. Can't anything go right for me?'' she complained in disgust. But she wasn't one to give up. She'd get rid of Emily, and Liza, if necessary, if it was the last thing she did.

Several times the next week Liza used the blond wig to go with Bonnie to the grocery store and once to the shopping mall. The realization that there would be no quick end to her problems made it difficult to continue to hide. When they ran into anyone the housekeeper knew, Bonnie used the story she'd made up earlier, that Liza was her niece come for a visit.

But they kept that secret from Nick.

On Wednesday, Emily called, and Liza told her about the phone call and their talk with Detective Ramsey. It didn't make either of them feel better. Then Emily asked how much longer Liza would be at the doctor's house, but she couldn't answer that question.

She wanted to stay as long as she could. It was going to be painful whenever she had to leave. So why not enjoy every minute until it became necessary?

Nick continued to be as loving as ever. And he hadn't pressed the issue about children. He seemed to have adopted the attitude that Liza had—one day at a time.

Liza was as happy as was possible in the circumstances. She worried about Emily, of course, but she reveled in Nick's love, and enjoyed getting out with Bonnie. She would've preferred that things continue as they were for a while longer.

On Thursday, however, she accompanied Bonnie to the grocery store and everything changed. One of Bonnie's friends stopped her for a chat, while Liza looked interestedly at some magazines.

"You don't know of anyone who wants a temporary job, do you?" the woman asked.

"What kind of job?" Bonnie asked.

"Well, you know my daughter runs the day care center at the hospital that all the employees use. It seems there's a flu epidemic going around, and half her staff is out sick. I'm going in tomorrow to help, but she'll still be shorthanded."

Liza's ears perked up. She loved children, in spite of not being able to have any. Why not spend a day or two working at the hospital? With her blond wig, no one seemed to recognize her.

"Aunt Bonnie, I could do that," Liza said, turning to the housekeeper.

"Oh, no, lovey!" Bonnie exclaimed. "Nick wouldn't want that."

Her friend stared at her curiously. "Why would Dr. Hathaway object? It would be wonderful if your niece could come. What was your name, dearie?"

Liza had to think fast. She and Bonnie hadn't bothered with a name when they'd made up the story. "Um, Liza. Liza Brown."

"I didn't know you had any Browns in your family, Bonnie," the woman said.

Liza answered before Bonnie could speak. She wasn't sure she'd come up with anything from her dazed expression. "No, but I, um, was briefly married," Liza added.

"Oh, of course. I'm surprised you kept the name," the woman said. Then smiling at her, she said, "So can I tell my daughter you'll be there in the morning?"

"Yes, if I can come at nine. I can't get there any earlier."

"And I'll have to pick you up at four-thirty," Bonnie said urgently. "So your daughter will probably want to get someone else, who can stay longer."

"She's so desperate, she'll take anyone," the woman said. "How about you, Bonnie? Want to help, too?"

"Maybe I'd better," she muttered, staring at Liza. "That way I can, uh, help out."

"Terrific! I'll call you tonight after I talk to my daughter." Then the woman pushed her cart down the aisle.

"Nick is going to kill us!" Bonnie whispered.

"We won't tell him, Bonnie. You can say you're helping out, and you know I'm not supposed to answer the phone. He'll never know."

"But, Liza, what if someone recognizes you?"

"I'm not nearly as famous as you think. Besides, the only ones I really have to hide from aren't here right now. And they sure wouldn't look for me in a day care center. It'll be fine, you'll see.''

''I certainly hope so,'' Bonnie said with a sigh.

Thirteen

When Nick came home that evening, he noticed both of the women in his household seemed nervous. Bonnie wouldn't meet his gaze, which wasn't a good sign.

"What's up?" he asked, watching both of them.

His housekeeper jumped, as if he'd scared her, and muttered "Nothing."

Liza smiled at him and moved into his embrace for a kiss. He was easily distracted by Liza's closeness, but he made a mental note to try to catch Bonnie alone and question her.

"Dinner will be ready in half an hour if you want to, you know, visit with Liza," Bonnie offered, still not looking at him. But he'd worry about what was going on later. Right now he could think of nothing but Liza.

"Good idea, Bonnie." He took Liza's hand and headed out of the kitchen.

"Wait a minute!" Liza protested, pulling back. He turned to stare at her. "You don't want to... talk?"

Liza sent him a teasing smile. "Of course I do, but it's nice to be asked and not taken for granted. You're getting a little spoiled."

"Oh, you think so?" he asked, his eyebrows rising as he pulled her against him again. But she was right. He had gotten spoiled. Having Liza welcome him home, spend the evening with him and the nights... Yeah, he was spoiled, all right, and he hoped it continued for the rest of his life.

That thought took him by surprise. Liza was more right then she'd realized. She'd charmed him right out of his decision to remain alone. He couldn't imagine a life without her now. Without realizing it, he was looking to the future with a smile on his face for the first time in four years.

He hadn't actually told Liza he loved her. He didn't want to make life difficult for her right now. She had too much to deal with. But he would. He wasn't going to let her go. He lowered his head and whispered an invitation in her ear that had her blushing.

Bonnie chuckled, sounding more normal. "Lovey, you'd better take him out of here before I get embarrassed."

Liza did as Bonnie suggested, tugging on Nick's hand. He didn't hesitate to follow her. He never would.

Once they were in the den with the door closed, Nick pulled her to him. "Do I need to ask permission to kiss you?"

Her answer was to cover his lips with hers, and all thought flew out of his head. He was being spoiled and he loved it.

The next morning, as Nick was leaving, Bonnie said, "Oh, Nick, I won't be home all day. I'm helping out a friend. So if you call and don't get an answer, don't worry."

Liza pretended to keep her gaze fixed on her scrambled eggs, but she tensed waiting for Nick's response. She and Bonnie had discussed when it would be best to tell him. They had decided to wait until he was walking out the door.

"What friend?" he asked as he gathered up his medical bag and briefcase.

"Marge Joyner."

He came to an abrupt halt. "What's wrong with Marge?"

"Nothing," Bonnie hurriedly said.

"But she doesn't work. Her daughter—" He broke off and frowned at his housekeeper. "I heard the day care needed help. Is that what you're doing?"

"Yes. I said I'd help out today."

Nick turned to Liza. "Will you be all right here alone?"

Liza raised one eyebrow, acting for all she was worth. "Of course. I won't answer the door or the phone. I figure I'll get a lot of writing done."

Still frowning, Nick leaned over and kissed her. "Okay, but be careful."

"I will."

When he left the house, the two women remained quiet until they heard his car leave the driveway.

Then Bonnie said, "Mercy, Liza, I thought I was going to break down and confess before he could leave. I'm too old for this."

"I'm sorry, Bonnie, but—but I want things to be normal so badly, and I don't think there's any danger to me, truly."

"I know, lovey. I wouldn't have agreed if I thought it would hurt you. The doctor tends to err on the side of caution."

"I know. I'm going upstairs and put on the wig. Then I'll be ready to go. I don't think it will matter if we get there a little early."

"Mercy, no. I expect we'll be greeted with open arms."

And they were. Liza looked at the room full of toddlers, her gaze twinkling. "Oh, Bonnie, aren't they darling?"

"That they are. I've been longing for Nick to— I mean, I'll feel like a grandmother if Nick ever— Well, yes, they are cute as can be."

A woman only a few years older than Liza rushed forward. "Oh, Mrs. Allen and Liza, is it? I'm so grateful you came. Mom's here, of course, but I had to send the only worker I had left home a few minutes ago. This flu epidemic is killing me!"

"Just tell us what you need us to do," Bonnie said,

setting her handbag on a nearby shelf. Liza did the same.

Soon both of them were on the floor, playing with the children, organizing games or supervising a group activity. Liza loved it.

After a lunch of peanut butter and jelly sandwiches, it was nap time for all the children, except one little girl about eighteen months old, who cried and cried. Liza offered to rock the baby so she wouldn't awaken the other children.

Settling in one of the rockers, Liza cuddled the little girl to her. One small hand reached for the shoulder-length blond hair. Liza gasped and started to remove the hand, but the baby seemed content to just hold on, so Liza relaxed against the back of the rocker and began singing softly.

The head of the center stared at her in surprise, and Liza changed to a hum. It hadn't occurred to her that her voice might be recognized.

Just as the baby was fading to sleep, the door to the nursery opened and two men entered, one carrying a local TV station video camera.

Liza searched for Bonnie, wondering what was going on. As she did so, the baby jerked awake and started crying again—and tugged on the wig.

Pandemonium reigned as the two men recognized Liza at once. The camera was turned on and pointed in her direction and the reporter rushed over to start asking questions. Liza tried to comfort the baby and pull the wig back on at the same time, ignoring the reporter.

Bonnie rushed to her side and told the men to stop filming.

They kept right on going.

"Please, you don't understand!" Liza said. "And you're upsetting the baby."

Within seconds, the other children were awakened, some crying. Marge, Bonnie's friend, added her efforts to her friend's, to get the men out of the day care center.

"We'll go as soon as Ms. Colton gives us an interview," the reporter bargained. "We came to film a story about the flu epidemic, but this is a lot better story."

Liza wanted to groan, but she tried to maintain her composure. Unfortunately, she really had no choice if they were to restore order to the day care. Besides, these were local reporters. No one who wanted to harm her would see the interview.

"All right, but only a brief one," she said. She handed the crying child to Bonnie. "Out in the hall," she told the crew. "You're upsetting the children."

When she returned to the day care a few minutes later, order had been restored, and she apologized to the director for the disturbance.

"It's all right. I hope you can stay. I wouldn't ask, but I don't have enough people as it is, Ms. Colton."

"Of course I can stay." They couldn't possibly put it on the news until six o'clock, so, she reasoned, everything would be fine.

Bonnie hurried to her side. "Is everything all right?

Did they promise to keep quiet about your being here?''

''Of course not, but I didn't tell them where I'm staying, and we'll have plenty of time to warn Nick.''

''Oh, mercy! He's going to kill us!''

Liza discovered how much she'd misjudged the situation when she and Bonnie tried to leave at four-thirty. With her blond wig firmly in place, she and the housekeeper stepped into the hall, only to discover the same reporter and cameraman waiting for them.

''Ms. Colton, I need to ask you some more questions. The entertainment shows want more information.''

Liza stared at the man with a microphone stuck beneath her nose. ''You got the interview for your local station.''

''Yeah, but I didn't know then they'd be interested. They're offering a lot of money to find out where you've been hiding!'' He grinned with enthusiasm, obviously expecting her to be thrilled about that information.

''No,'' Liza said firmly and tried to move away.

''Come on, Ms. Colton. We'll just follow you if you don't cooperate.''

The truth of his statement struck her. Her safe haven would be gone. And if the news went out of Saratoga Springs, it was bound to be seen by the wrong people. She might even put Nick and Bonnie in danger.

She didn't want to do that.

Tears pooled in her eyes. "I'll give you a brief interview if you'll follow me to the airport."

"You won't tell anyone else, will you?" the cameraman asked, obviously anxious to protect his exclusive story.

"No, I won't tell anyone," she promised even as she felt Bonnie squeeze her arm.

"We'll take you to the airport, then," the reporter promised.

Liza realized they weren't going to let her out of sight, so she might as well make use of them. "Thank you, I appreciate that. If you'll just give me a moment, I need to tell the lady I can't come back tomorrow."

After they nodded, she pushed Bonnie back into the nursery, closing the door behind her.

"You're not leaving, lovey?" Bonnie cried.

"I don't have a choice. If this story is going national, then I might endanger you and Nick. I have to go."

"Without even telling Nick goodbye?" Bonnie asked, disbelief in her voice.

Liza shook her head. "I don't have a choice, Bonnie. Tell him...everything is my fault. You tried to convince me not to come today. And—" There was so much she wanted to say, but she couldn't. "Tell him thank you." She hugged Bonnie, feeling like she was leaving her mother.

Then she slipped from the room, leaving Bonnie inside with tears in her eyes.

*   *   *

Nick had left his office early because he had a patient in the hospital whom he needed to check on. He thought about Bonnie working there today and thought he'd stop by afterward to see if she was still at work. He smiled. Maybe she was discovering she enjoyed little ones so she'd be enthusiastic when he convinced Liza to stay with him, to have a future, with a lot of kids. He smiled as he hurried to his patient, eager to return to Liza.

When he reached the nursery, he opened the door. There were only a couple of children left waiting for their parents. But what immediately caught his eye was Bonnie, sitting in a rocker, another lady patting her shoulder as she cried.

"Bonnie! What happened?"

"Oh, Nick, I'm so sorry! I thought it would be all right, but the wig came off, and those reporters were all over her. She said it would be okay. No one would pay any attention, but—but they sold the story to national television—and Liza left!"

Nick's heart skipped a beat. He couldn't believe it. She wouldn't leave without talking to him. Besides, she was supposed to be back at the house.

"Of course she didn't leave, Bonnie. She's at home."

Bonnie sadly shook her head.

"But—but she came here?"

Bonnie nodded.

Even so, he protested again. "She wouldn't leave. She was probably trying to throw everyone off the

trail. She'll be at home, waiting for us. Come on, let's
go. She's probably scared.''

He took Bonnie's hand and pulled her from the day
care center out to the parking lot and his car.

He got Bonnie inside and hurried out of the parking
lot, praying he was right, that Liza would be home
waiting for them.

It was the only way he could keep from falling
apart.

Much to the reporter's disgust, the only information
Liza gave him was that she'd enjoyed her stay in the
hotel. She figured that could only help the hotel.
Other than that, she used her credit card to buy a
ticket to New York, and refused any other questions.
Then she disappeared into a special lounge until the
flight was called.

The airline personnel loaded all the other passengers on the plane. Then, at the last minute, Liza took
her seat.

Thank goodness she'd taken her purse to the day
care with her. She'd considered leaving it at Nick's,
assuming she wouldn't need anything, but something
had made her decide at the last minute to carry it.

When the short flight to New York was over and
she'd picked up the luggage she'd sent when she'd
first gone to Nick's, she hurried from the airport,
grabbing a taxi and getting away.

She went to her apartment at once, greeting the
doorman, excusing herself from answering his questions. In her apartment, she checked everything. Then

she exchanged a few things for what she had in the suitcase and donned a wig her mother had insisted she buy when she cut her hair. It was approximately her hair color but it was long. Liza took the time to braid the long hair, taking away its fullness.

In jeans and a T-shirt, she hoped she'd blend into the crowds. Her bank was only a few stops from her apartment. She managed to get there before it closed and withdrew a large amount of money.

Then she checked into a modest hotel, using the name Liza Bonney. Once she was shown to her room, she tipped the bellhop and locked the door behind him.

Then she collapsed on the bed and shed the tears she'd been holding back ever since she'd left Saratoga Springs. Tears that mourned her departure, her loss of Nick, her loss of Bonnie, her loss of all that mattered.

Nick was furious.

Liza wasn't at his home, waiting for him. Running into his embrace, her lips raised for a kiss.

Bonnie tearfully confessed what had happened. Nick couldn't rail at her. She'd made mistakes, but Liza had insisted. Nick himself hadn't been very good at resisting Liza, and Bonnie hadn't really understood the situation. He should've told her.

But Liza…she knew. She risked what they'd had, knowing how dangerous it was. Knowing how much he— She had to have known how much he loved her. And she destroyed it.

As his anger eased, the ache in his heart took over. And the fear. He wanted to know she was safe. He wanted to know where to find her. He called her apartment and left a message for her to call him.

Sleep didn't come easily that night. When he got up to go to the office, he couldn't help remembering waking up with Liza beside him. Her clothes still hung in his closet. Her toiletries were in his bathroom. Her scent was still on his bedsheets.

Bonnie wouldn't even meet his gaze, just as she hadn't the day before. There was no mystery today. He knew what was going on.

"Bonnie, it's not your fault," he finally said. "I hadn't warned you how—how serious the situation was."

"But I knew you wouldn't like it," she said with a sniff.

Nick shook his head. "I wish— Maybe I am a little dictatorial. I should have told you the truth so you could make the right decision, instead of expecting absolute obedience. So I share the blame. Don't worry. We'll find her. She'll be safe."

He had no taste for breakfast, so he hurried out, hoping work would take his mind off Liza. He'd talked to Detective Ramsey last night, and the man had promised to let him know if they had any word from Liza.

Because he'd skipped breakfast, he got to work half an hour early, startling his office staff.

"Oh, Doctor," his nurse called as she heard him

come in. She rushed into his office. "You just missed a call from Ms. Colton!"

"Where is she? Did she leave a number?"

"No, sir. She said to tell you she was fine, that was all."

"Damn it, Missy, why didn't you ask for a number?" Nick shouted. The stunned look on his nurse's face brought him back to reality. "Sorry, Missy, I— I was worried about her."

"Yes, sir. Did you know she was still here? I had no idea. I can't believe she stayed at the hotel without telling anyone? There's a big article in the paper, on the front page. Did you know?"

Nick wanted to shout that yes, he knew. She was his. She'd been in his house, in his arms, in his bed. But he couldn't. That would be foolish. "Uh, no. I saw her at the hotel, so maybe there's nothing else to know."

"How exciting!" She sighed. "I knew she couldn't have been staying with you, or you would've gotten me that autograph. Oh, well. Maybe she'll come back and I'll get another chance."

"I hope so," he assured her. Then he picked up the patient charts waiting on his desk for his morning appointments, hoping Missy would take the hint.

When she'd gone, he called Detective Ramsey. "Have you heard anything?" he asked at once.

"Have you?"

"She called my office before I got here. Said she was all right, but she didn't leave a number."

"The NYPD went to her apartment. The doorman

said she showed up there, in a hurry. But he didn't see her leave. He went up with the officers and knocked on the door, but she didn't answer. The doorman decided to open the door for them because he was worried about her. There were signs of hurried packing, but she wasn't there."

Nick sighed in frustration. "You think that man will be back?"

"Yeah. The police are staking out the apartment."

"Good. Keep me informed," he said before hanging up.

Nick stared blindly across his office. He hadn't intended to let Liza go. He'd believed he could hold her close, protect her, keep her forever. But in a split second, she'd gone.

With a dispirited sigh, he called Bonnie. He knew she was worried. He had to let her know that Liza had called.

"But why didn't she call here?" Bonnie asked, tears in her voice.

"Because she didn't want us to know where she was," he answered harshly, unhappy to admit that out loud. "Look, Bonnie, she's safe. She's not dumb. She knows how serious her situation is."

"I miss her," Bonnie sobbed.

"Yeah, me, too." And he hung up the phone. Miss her? What an understatement. He was having difficulty breathing.

He'd thought he'd loved Daphne when he'd married her. But he hadn't loved her even half as much as he loved Liza. By the time the marriage went sour, he hadn't cared at all.

But he knew he'd long for Liza for the rest of his life. For a few days, that dream of a happy family had burned brightly in his heart.

But as long as Liza was missing, that dream was dead.

There would never be anyone else but her.

Fourteen

———

The next morning Liza dressed and went out to find a coffee shop near the hotel. Having learned her lesson about skipping meals, she forced herself to eat, but her plate was still half full when she paid her bill and slipped out to mingle with the crowds on the street.

She hopped on a bus, not even caring where it was going. She had to call Bonnie, to be sure Nick didn't blame his housekeeper for what had happened. Fifteen blocks later, she got off and found a pay phone.

"Bonnie?" she said when the housekeeper answered. "It's Liza."

"Lord have mercy, I know that, lovey! Where are you? Are you all right?"

"I'm fine. Nick didn't— He didn't get upset with you, did he?"

"No, lovey, he was wonderful. He blamed himself for not telling me how serious everything was. He's such a good man. And he wants to talk to you."

Liza held back a sob. "I—I can't, Bonnie. I'd start crying. He would only worry. I promise I'm all right. Maybe—maybe after that man is caught, I can come for a visit."

"You call us if you need anything, you hear? Anything at all. Call us whenever you want."

"I will."

Then she took the lonely ride back to her hotel. Nearby, she found a store and bought some paper and pens so she could continue to write her music. It was the only thing that would keep her from going crazy.

Nick had thought the worst had occurred when Liza left, but he learned differently the next morning.

When he came downstairs for breakfast, Bonnie had a strange look on her face.

"What's wrong?"

She nodded to the paper beside his plate.

He sat down and was reaching for it when the doorbell rang.

"Sit down," Bonnie said in a matter-of-fact tone. "We're not answering it."

Nick sank back into his chair, staring openmouthed at his gentle, kind housekeeper. "Why?"

She nodded to the newspaper again. "You'll see."

He unfolded the paper to stare at his own picture, alongside a publicity shot of Liza.

"Now do you understand?" Bonnie asked.

"They found out Liza stayed here?"

"Yes, and there's several reporters on the lawn."

"Damn!" Nick got up and lifted one slat of the blinds to peer outside. Bonnie was right. There were several men with cameras leaning against their cars. He walked back to the phone and dialed Detective Ramsey's number.

"Detective, there are some reporters on my lawn. Can anything be done?"

"Well, sir, we can move them to the sidewalk. That's the best we can do. You might want to talk to them, tell them she stayed to get well and then left. And you have no knowledge of her present location. That might get rid of them faster than anything I can do."

Nick thanked him. After explaining to Bonnie what he was going to do, he followed the detective's suggestion. To his surprise, after several persistent questions, to which he gave the same answer, he returned to the house and watched from the window as they drove away.

Then he sat down. "Is breakfast ready?"

"You want to eat?" his housekeeper asked in surprise.

"Of course I want to eat."

"It's ready," she said and took a filled plate out of the oven. "Aren't you going to read the article?"

"Since the title says 'Famous Singer in Love Nest

with Doctor', I doubt if it would make me feel good.''
He took a bite of eggs and chewed steadily, wondering why they tasted like cardboard.

Bonnie sat down at the table to eat also, remaining silent. She'd told him last night about Liza's call.

About her refusal to talk to him. He'd tossed and turned all night, his stomach filled with something like battery acid.

He hoped Liza wouldn't see this article. Hopefully, the New York papers had more important things to cover than some sleazy story. He hoped his neighbors wouldn't read it either.

An hour later, he knew everyone he'd ever known had read it. Because it seemed they all tried to call him.

Nick sighed. He could live with that. After all, things couldn't get much worse, so he'd simply wait it out.

Until Missy appeared at the door of his office. ''Doctor, there's a lady on the phone demanding to talk to you.''

''No calls, Missy.''

''But she says she's your ex-wife.''

Okay, so maybe things could get worse. ''Okay, Missy, what line is she on?''

''Line three, Doctor.'' Then she withdrew, closing the door behind her.

''Daphne, what do you want?'' he growled into the phone.

''Well,'' she huffed, ''it's nice to hear your voice, too, Nick, darling.''

He didn't respond.

"You're not being very friendly," she went on.

"You've got five seconds before I hang up."

"If you want to see your son, you won't do that."

Nick's heart double-clutched. "My what?"

"Do you remember that last time we shared a romantic moment?"

He remembered. They'd had separate rooms for six months, until she'd slipped into his room late one night and seduced him.

His reaction wasn't what she expected. The next morning he'd told her he was divorcing her.

"I remember," he finally said.

"Well, we created little Timmy. He's three years and two months old. Can you add, darling?"

Nick felt as if he'd been broadsided. A child? But how could he be sure. It was Daphne, after all. He couldn't trust her—not before, not now. "Has he been tested?" he asked. "I'll give my DNA to a clinic to be sure."

"You doubt me?" She sounded affronted. "You think I'd lie about something this important?"

"Why not? You've been lying to me for years."

"Darling, you were angry with me. I thought I'd wait until you cooled off. But I didn't expect you to find someone else. You've kept to yourself all this time."

Like a lightbulb going off in his head, Nick now knew what had provoked her call. Daphne didn't want him, but she didn't want anyone else to have him.

But he had no intention of accepting her word for

anything. She'd lied too many times, in particular about her activities while married to him. There had been men, a number of men.

He wanted proof.

"Well, if you insist, we'll do the testing, darling, but it takes time, and I've already visited with a charming reporter this morning. I'm afraid you may lose patients when they realize you're not taking responsibility for your own child."

"Damn you, Daphne, there will be tests. And if they show the child is mine, I'll pay child support. But I don't want you in my life in any way."

"So you've fallen for the little songbird? Isn't she a little drab? You could do better, darling."

"No, I couldn't. And, Daphne, if the test shows someone else is the father, you'll hear from my lawyer for defamation of character." Then he slammed down the phone.

And buried his face in his hands.

Liza found the article buried on page nine of the *New York Post*. Her publicity photo was beside a picture of Nick. Wanting to keep his picture, she called down to the desk to borrow a pair of scissors. While she waited for the bellhop, she scanned the article.

And stopped breathing.

Nick had a son? A son he didn't know about? And his ex-wife wanted to reunite with him?

When the bellhop knocked on the door, Liza answered it, not even aware tears were streaming down her cheeks.

"Miss, are you all right?"

"Fine," she said with a gulp. She handed him a tip and took the scissors, closing the door while he still stood there.

Finally she admitted to herself that she'd hoped to return to Nick when it was safe. She'd hoped he'd marry her, even though they couldn't have children. Maybe he'd consider adoption. She'd lulled herself to sleep for the past four days by telling herself they still had a future.

But Nick already had a child. And a chance to teach him to fish. To share the important moments in life with him. To provide a real home, a mother and a father.

She couldn't lie to herself anymore. There was no future for her and Nick.

Loud knocking on the door distracted her. "Ma'am? Ma'am, please open the door! Ma'am?"

She couldn't imagine what was wrong, but she opened the door after looking through the peephole. It was the hotel manager.

"Yes?"

"Ma'am, are you all right?" The man was staring at her, his eyes darting from her feet to her head, a frantic look on his face.

"I'm fine," she assured him and tried to close the door.

"Ma'am, are you aware you're crying?"

"Of course I'm crying," she snapped, unable to think of anything but Nick.

"But you said you were all right."

"I am! Just leave me alone!"

Again she tried to slam the door, but the man stuck in his foot. "Uh, ma'am, have you finished with the scissors?"

"That's what your visit is about? You need the scissors back?"

"No, ma'am...but when a person is upset...well, there's no telling what they'll do."

Liza stared at him. Then all of a sudden she realized what the manager was saying: he was afraid she'd commit suicide with his scissors.

"I'm not— Here are your damn scissors," she snapped, grabbing the scissors and slapping them into his hands. "Now, go away!"

"So sorry," he murmured, backing out of the room.

She slammed the door successfully this time and collapsed back on the bed. Then she had a long talk with herself, reminding herself of the promise she'd made days ago: she'd walk away from Nick, allow him to have his dream of children.

When the phone rang, Bonnie rushed to it. It could be those pesky reporters—whom she'd get rid of fast enough—but it could also be Liza.

"May I speak to Liza, please?"

Well, this was a new approach, she decided grimly. "It's not going to do you any good to ask for her. You know she's not here."

"Wait! I'm— She gave me this number. When did she leave?"

Bonnie debated what to do. Finally, she said, "Who is this?"

Silence was her answer.

Just as she started to hang up the receiver, the woman spoke. "I'm Emma Logan."

"Her cousin?"

"Yes. Please tell me when she left."

"A few days ago. I guess it was Friday. Some reporters found out she was here and she had to hide again. Are you all right?"

"Yes. But she said she'd call when…if she left."

"She called here and said she was safe."

"Is she in New York?"

"Yes, but—" She heard a door open behind her and realized Nick had come downstairs. "Just a minute." Then she held out the phone for Nick. "It's Liza's cousin."

Nick grabbed the phone. "Emily, are you all right?"

"I'm fine, but what about Liza? She said she'd call if she had to leave."

Nick worried about the tone of Emily's words. She sounded frantic. "Are you sure you're safe? I think the police would keep your location secret if you need help."

"No! No, I'm fine, but I want Liza to be safe. It's not safe for me to call her apartment…."

"She's not there anyway," Nick revealed. "We've called. All we know is that she's in one of the hundreds of hotels in the city."

"Why did she leave?"

Nick swallowed. "She decided she couldn't stay. The reporters found her at the hospital and she didn't want to lead them back here."

"At the hospital? Is she still sick? I thought—"

"She's fine. She was volunteering at the child-care center, wearing a wig."

"That long one her mom made her buy?"

Nick wondered if he'd just found a key to Liza's disguise. "What color was it?"

"About the same color as her own hair, but it falls halfway down her back."

"No," he answered calmly, "she was using a blond wig."

"Look, if she calls, would you please tell her to call me?"

"Sure. But will you do the same? Tell her to call me?" he asked.

"I'll talk to her about it."

That was the best answer he could get. He knew Emily wouldn't tell him where Liza was if and when she found out. But he couldn't believe Liza had forgotten her cousin. Nothing had been more important to Liza than Emily's safety.

It made him worry about her even more.

Emily returned to the café, her break over. But she couldn't hide her concern. Toby Atkins, having coffee on his usual stool, immediately asked, "What's wrong?"

In her concern over Liza, Emily had forgotten

Toby's presence. "Oh! What? Nothing. Nothing's wrong."

"I thought maybe you had some bad news. You know, about your problems back home."

She'd told a sob story about the death of her fiancé back home, her need to get away. "Uh, no. I was calling my...sister. She's got a cold." She worked up a casual smile.

He nodded and said, "I see." Then he surprised her by reaching out to cover her hands on the counter. "You know I'll help you with anything, don't you, Emma?"

She knew. In the beginning, she'd thought that was a good thing. But now she realized she'd gone too far. Toby had a crush on her. She didn't feel that way about him, though, and didn't want to mislead him.

Which was a shame. But for some reason, take-charge guys appealed to her. Probably because that's how her dad was. Joe Colton always led, never followed.

"I know, Toby, and I appreciate it. But I'm fine. More coffee?"

He shook his head. "I'd better make my rounds." He stood and donned his cowboy hat, part of the uniform he wore. "The sheriff wants me to serve some warrants."

"Be careful," she said with a smile.

She only prayed Liza was doing the same.

Even though Liza believed she had no future with Nick, she couldn't turn loose. She traveled around the city, using different pay phones to check her messages and to call Bonnie. It nearly killed her to ignore Nick's message, left as her physician following up on his patient, no doubt because he could risk calling no other way. She didn't have the nerve to call him back or even ask Bonnie about him or about Nick's little boy...or his former wife.

Bonnie had frankly told her she hated Daphne, but Liza knew the kind woman would put up with anyone for the sake of Nick's child.

She hadn't even realized she'd fallen into a pattern, calling about ten o'clock each day, when Nick would be at work. And not calling on the weekends.

She listened to the first ring, her heart beating a little faster to be so close to Nick. When his voice answered the phone, she almost began to cry. She loved the sound of his voice.

"Hello? Hello? Liza, is that you?"

"Nick," she said in a hushed whisper.

"Liza, come back. I can't—"

"Nick, I can't. It would be too dangerous for you. I want you and Bonnie to be safe."

At least he hadn't forgotten about her. He cared about her safety. The relief of knowing that filled her eyes with tears.

"Ramsey called. The man came back to your apartment. The police chased him and he ran into the street. He was hit by a taxi.... Liza, he's dead."

"Are they sure?" she asked, unable to believe at least some of the danger was gone.

"I'm sure. They showed me a picture. It was him. Come back, Liza."

"I can't. There are other— I have to think!" Her stomach was churning and she knew she was going to be sick.

She hung up the phone but before she could figure out where to go, she doubled over and lost what breakfast she'd had that morning. Though she was embarrassed, she took a tissue and wiped her face.

She hoped she wasn't getting sick. She had to decide what to do about her situation. She loved Nick, but she couldn't make him give up his child. And she feared his ex-wife might demand marriage as the price for his child.

The first thing she had to do was change hotels, just to be sure, to move from one which thought she'd wanted to commit suicide with their scissors. Then she'd figure out what to do next.

Liza left the hotel to call Emily at what should be her break time. After a brief conversation to tell Emily she was okay, Liza called her uncle's Prosperino home. The housekeeper answered.

"Inez, it's Liza. Is Uncle Joe there?"

"Child, everyone's worried about you! Where are you? Even your mother has called for you."

"I know. I'm in New York City. Uncle Joe?"

"Just a minute, hon. I'll see if I can find him."

Liza waited patiently for Joe to come to the phone.

"Liza? Is that you?" her uncle's deep, strong voice filled her ears and she sighed with relief.

"Yes, Uncle Joe. Are you all right?"

"Considering the circumstances, I guess so. How about you? And who's this doctor?"

"Just a doctor, Uncle. Nothing to worry about."

"Are you still touring?"

"No, I got so upset about Emily I didn't take care of myself. It will be a while before I can sing again." Then she switched the topic. "What have they found out about who tried to kill you?"

"Not much. I'm more concerned about Emily. I'm afraid...I'm afraid we may have lost her," he finished with a sob.

Liza felt terrible to let him suffer when she knew Emily was all right...for the moment. "Don't give up hope, Uncle Joe. We'll find her."

"Come home, Liza. If you're not touring, you can—"

"No, I can't. You know how Mom is." She knew Joe would understand that inference. Everyone knew how her mother pushed her career.

"Okay, but call me again, okay?"

"I will. Take care of yourself."

Fifteen

Though Liza had been gone for two weeks, Nick remembered the few days he'd held her close as if it were another world. How eagerly he'd come home each evening. How close he'd been to his dream life.

Now he seldom smiled. Occasionally, Liza called the house, but she'd become unpredictable about her times. He couldn't stay home all day just to hear her voice. She never talked long, according to Bonnie. It's hard to have a long conversation when you don't reveal anything about yourself.

Not that his days had been boring since Liza's departure. He'd tracked down the reporter who had interviewed Daphne and warned him that the information she'd given the reporter was false. Then he called the editor at the paper and warned him that if he printed any more of Daphne's lies, he'd be sued.

His lawyer was certainly staying busy...and getting richer all the time.

Then Nick had submitted the DNA sample, but, as he'd suspected, Daphne had disappeared without letting her child be tested. He'd never even seen the boy.

So he'd hired a private investigator to find them.

He wanted to hire someone to search for Liza, too, but he feared it might endanger her. Besides, she knew where he was and didn't want to see him. He'd hoped when he told her that the man who'd scared her was dead that she'd come back home. Instead, she'd hung up on him.

"Doctor?"

He looked up. "Yes, Missy?"

"Everything's wrapped up here. Aren't you going home?"

"Yeah, sure. Go ahead and lock up. I'll see you tomorrow."

She nodded and turned away, but not before he saw the concern in her eyes. It was nice to know that his staff cared about his happiness. But they couldn't help.

The phone rang and he picked up the receiver.

"Nick, are you coming home?"

"Bonnie? Of course I am."

"Good, because Liza's going to be on television!"

"What? What's happened?" His heart was thumping overtime, fearing she might be in more trouble.

"I was checking out the television schedule for tonight and found a benefit program from Carnegie Hall. And she's listed as one of the entertainers.'' His housekeeper sounded breathless, like she'd been running.

"Is it live?" he demanded, already mentally figuring how soon he could get to New York City.

"No, it's taped, it says right here."

It was enough to make a man want to cry, he decided as he gathered himself. "Okay, I'll be home in a few minutes."

Bonnie had dinner waiting, but he wasn't interested. He put a new tape in the VCR, then he paced the floor, waiting for the program to start.

It wasn't until Liza, with her quiet beauty and grace, took center stage that he sat down and stared at the television. His heart melted all over again as he watched her. She sang one of the songs from her first album. Bonnie had gone out and bought it after Liza left.

"It's so good to see her," his housekeeper whispered.

When she finished, they went to commercial after announcing Liza would sing again.

"I wonder what she'll sing next?" Bonnie asked.

Nick didn't answer. He didn't care what she sang, as long as he could see her. The only thing better would be to hold her against him...and never let go.

Meredith watched the production in her husband's presence. He didn't often share the same room with her, and he never shared her bed. Not since she'd announced her pregnancy, not realizing he was sterile.

After Liza left the stage, she suggested, "We should call Liza and congratulate her." She still didn't believe Joe didn't know how to reach his niece.

"I don't know where she is," he answered gruffly. "She called from New York, but I don't know where exactly. Apparently she's not living in her apartment."

"Why wouldn't she be in her apartment?"

"Why the concern all of a sudden, Meredith?"

He stared at her, but she pretended everything was all right. Her acting skills were even better than Liza's. She thought her niece's death might be a necessity, but Liza wasn't top priority. Emily was the key. She'd told the idiot she'd hired to concentrate on Emily.

"You two don't get along much anymore, do you?" Joe's question broke into her thoughts.

Meredith snapped her head around. Always stick as close to the truth as possible. "No, not really. That happens when children grow up. They get involved in their own lives, you know."

And sisters, too. She'd been abandoned by her own sister. The real Meredith had married Joe and become wealthy, but she'd never bothered about her twin. She deserved what she got.

The only problem was she was out there somewhere. Could she still have amnesia after nine years? Meredith desperately wanted to know where the real

Meredith was hiding. She wasn't going to lose her position…whatever it took.

She'd gone into town again today and talked with the man she'd hired to locate Meredith. He'd found nothing. Unable to bear the tension, she'd snapped and fired him with no finesse.

Then she'd made an appointment with the best-known firm in the country. She should have hired them to find Emily, too. But there would be a lot of police scrutiny when Emily was…eliminated. When her own sister disappeared, it wouldn't be noticed. No one would care about a mentally ill old woman.

She leaned back against the sofa. Yes, she was shortly going to have everything under control. And Liza was no dummy. When Emily turned up dead, she'd know not to say anything.

Even if she did, no one would believe her.

With a satisfied smile on her face, she settled back to watch the rest of the show.

Liza watched her appearance on television by herself, huddled under the covers in her new hotel room. She'd checked in yesterday, before anyone would be reminded of her appearance by the show she'd recorded months ago. Even though the man who'd been after her was now dead, she didn't want to take a chance returning to her apartment. Not just yet.

Was Nick watching? Was he missing her? Their time together had seemed so real, seemed that it would last forever. A tear slid down her cheek. She wouldn't cry, she insisted to herself.

She thought about the news that the man chasing her had died. And she thought about returning to Saratoga Springs. But she couldn't make up her mind. She needed to get well. She was so tired lately and she threw up sometimes when she first woke up. She could hear Nick's voice, warning her to take care of herself.

Galvanized by that thought, she called an outpatient clinic at a nearby hospital and made an appointment for the next morning.

It was dangerous doing so after her appearance on television, but with the wig and dark glasses, she didn't think she'd be recognized. She certainly wasn't going to return to Nick sick again. If she ever did.

Liza settled into a chair in the doctor's cubicle. They'd run several tests earlier, and she'd waited in a very uncomfortable chair for two hours to get the results.

"I need more iron, don't I?" she asked, trying to appear cheerful, when what she really wanted to do was crawl into a bed and sleep for days.

The doctor stared at her. "That will certainly be included in what I prescribe. However, it's not the main, uh, diagnosis."

Something about his expression put fear in her heart. "You mean...I have cancer?"

He looked startled. "Oh, no, not at all, Mrs...." he paused to look down at her paperwork. "Ms. Bonney, it's not anything like that. I hope it's good news. You're pregnant."

Liza didn't hesitate for a minute. "No, Doctor, I'm sorry. You must have misdiagnosed. I can't get pregnant."

"And why do you think that?"

She told him the diagnosis made by two separate doctors.

Instead of suggesting different tests, as she expected, he shook his head. "Ms. Bonney, they never said it was impossible. In this case, miracles do happen."

Liza stared at him as his words sank in. "You mean…I'm really pregnant?" Her voice rose, hysteria creeping in.

"Calm down. It's important for you to remain calm and happy. We want this baby to arrive healthy."

"There's something wrong with my baby?" she demanded, leaning forward. She found it hard enough to believe his diagnosis, much less a happy outcome.

"You're an alarmist, aren't you?" he asked, frowning. "I don't see any difficulties if you follow instructions."

"Of course I will! Tell me what to do. I'll do whatever it takes. I'll— When is the baby due?"

"You're only three weeks along. It's good that you came in so early. I have some pamphlets for you to read, and I'll prescribe some prenatal vitamins for you. You can get them at our pharmacy. Do you need help paying?"

"No, I can pay," she said, her mind on other things.

"We also have a store connected to the hospital

with donated clothes for pregnant women. You don't need them yet, but I want you to be aware of the assistance we can provide.''

Liza stared at him. Pregnancy clothes! She never thought she'd need them. Joy rose in her. She and Nick— Nick was going to have a child.

Then she remembered. He already had a child— and probably a wife by now. Lately she hadn't been calling as much, because she had nothing to say, and because she didn't want to hear that Nick and Daphne had remarried.

Her child, her precious child, wouldn't have a father. Not a father who lived with him, who was there for him...who taught him to fish.

Tears filled her eyes. It didn't matter, she told herself. She'd love her child more than any mother ever could. She'd—

''Ms. Bonney, are you all right?'' the doctor hurriedly asked. ''I didn't mean to upset you.''

''No, no, Doctor, I'm fine,'' she said, hurriedly blinking her eyes to dispel the moisture.

''Good. Now, here are the pamphlets and a prescription for the vitamins. And I'd like to see you back here in four weeks. Make an appointment with the nurse before you leave.''

''Yes, thank you, Doctor.'' Liza took the papers from him and tried to maintain calm while she escaped his gaze.

Such conflicting emotions filling her made control difficult. She was ecstatic about her baby. And devastated that Nick wouldn't be involved.

Without thinking, she hailed a cab as soon as she got outside the hospital. She had to be alone as soon as possible.

"Where to, lady?"

She named an intersection near her hotel and sat back, her mind buzzing with the possibilities.

"Hey, you look like that singer!" the cabbie exclaimed, catching her attention.

She gulped and strived for nonchalance. "Yeah, I've heard that before. I wish."

"You can't sing?" he asked.

"No, not a note. If I could, do you think I'd come to this place?" she asked in derision, gesturing to the hospital they were pulling away from.

He chuckled. "I guess not. Those stars always have a special room, lots of service. Us poor schnooks make do with long lines. Ah, must be the life."

"Yeah," she agreed and stared out the window.

Toby Atkins dropped by Annie Summers's antique store. Sometimes Emma worked there on her days off from the café. He always told her she needed to do something fun on her off days. But she said she loved antiques.

He frowned. That was only one unusual thing about Emma. For a woman who was supposedly burying her sorrow, she was awfully jumpy.

Anytime he mentioned a stranger in town, she pretended not to listen, but she grew real still until he identified the person.

He figured she was a runaway. That'd be the lesser

of the two evils, he reasoned. Because he also had a suspicion she might be the sweet young thing involved in a car theft con in some nearby towns.

But he couldn't believe that—not when he was around Emma, at least.

He wandered in and smiled at Annie. She was a single mother, pretty, sweet, but she didn't draw him like Emma did. "Emma working today?"

"Hi, Toby. Yes, she is, but she's gone to look at Mrs. Yardley's china. She wants to sell it and Emma knows more about china than I do."

"Isn't that strange?" he asked softly, watching Annie.

She looked away, rubbing a spot on the antique sideboard beside her. Shrugging her shoulders, she said, "Not really. A lot of people know more than you'd think."

"When will she be back?"

"Anytime now. She's been gone a couple of hours."

As if on cue, the front door jangled and Emma returned, her hands full of small boxes. Toby hurried over to help her. He stopped worrying about Emma's past. He was enjoying her too much in the present.

It wasn't easy to do, but Nick arranged a month's vacation for himself. Normally he would take a week when he was feeling burned out, and after a week, he was always back on the job, tending his patients.

This time, however, the vacation wasn't about burnout. It was about finding Liza. About getting his life back on track. About building his future with the woman he loved.

He'd cleared up the mess with Daphne. The P.I. he'd hired had found her and the little boy and taken pictures of the two of them. He'd also made pictures of a man, one Nick didn't know, with them. The boy, Timmy, looked like the man.

But Nick hadn't depended on what his eyes told him. He'd contacted his lawyer and had papers served on Daphne, demanding a paternity test. She'd agreed to the tests, but she pleaded with Nick not to sue her.

"Okay, I'll agree to no lawsuits. Just get the tests done."

"Why? You already know he's not yours," she snapped. "I don't want to go to the trouble."

"You'd prefer to go to court? To reveal what you've done?"

"Nick, you're being mean!"

"Yeah. So are you going to submit DNA for the boy?"

"Oh, all right!"

He'd gotten the results back on Tuesday. They were negative, as he'd expected. So he'd found friends to cover any patients who couldn't be cancelled or any emergencies that came up for the next month. He was catching a plane for New York City this evening.

He'd talked to Detective Ramsey but he couldn't give Nick much information. They'd traced the calls, but they'd all been from pay phones around the city.

He suggested leaving a message on Liza's apartment phone, asking her to meet him.

Nick hoped so.

But he was considering hiring a P.I., too. Detective Ramsey had recommended a firm in New York City.

He hurried home after his last patient, excitement building in him. He'd told himself it would take time and require patience, but at least he was finally doing something to bring Liza back into his life.

The love he felt for her was as strong today as it had been the last time he'd seen her. He believed he was a one-woman man, and his one woman was Liza Colton. He'd revise his idea of the perfect future. If she wanted to continue with her career, he'd agree.

As long as she always returned when she finished singing.

That was the important thing.

Sixteen

Liza's indecision was immediately gone. She was going to Saratoga Springs to tell Nick that she was pregnant. She wasn't going to ask for more than he could give, but he had to know about their baby.

Her hand slipped to her stomach, cradling her secret. She'd been making plans in her head, dreaming of the perfect place to raise a child. A house in the country, or in a small town. Somewhere quiet but with cultural advantages. A place just like Saratoga Springs.

But, of course, she couldn't go there if Nick had other plans.

She dismissed the sadness that welled up in her. There were other small towns, and she'd find one.

She jumped up from the bed, then reeled back

down. Fast movement and babies didn't seem to go together. Shaking her head, she rose more slowly the next time.

So. If she was going to go, why not now?

After looking up the number, she called the airlines and found one seat available in first class.

Pulling on jeans and a sweatshirt and throwing some clothes in a large shoulder bag, she hurried downstairs and hailed a taxi. In minutes she was on her way to the airport.

When she arrived, she heard the boarding call. "Last call for flight number 48 to Albany, Saratoga Springs and Burlington. All passengers must board now."

Liza raced for the gate weaving her way through the crowds. When she finally sat down in her assigned seat she was aware that her jeans weren't as comfortable as they used to be.

Would Nick be able to tell? Would he guess her secret before she told him? She chuckled at her ridiculous fears. She couldn't even tell when she looked in the mirror. But she spent the short flight obsessing on that anyway.

When the plane landed, she anxiously entered the airport. She had Nick on her mind. The excitement zinging through her veins was almost more than she could bear.

With no luggage to claim, she hurried down the hallway toward the front of the airport, where she'd find a cab. Though she was rushing, she automatically took in the people she passed. It had become habit.

Suddenly, she threw on the brakes as a tall, handsome man with a cleft in his chin hurried past.

"Nick!" she shouted, unable to keep quiet.

There he stood, a few yards away, with a suitcase in his hand. Suitcase? And he was headed for the check-in counter. He was leaving! No, no, he couldn't—

He barely slowed down, throwing a backward glance over his shoulder until he saw her.

He came to a complete halt, staring at her as if he thought she was an illusion. Then he hurriedly looked around him to see if they'd drawn any attention.

Liza's heart fell. He was worried about his reputation. Those awful stories in the newspapers must have caused him problems.

Even as she worried about his reaction, he reached her, but instead of pulling her into his arms, he stood, rigidly staring at her. "What are you doing here?"

She'd hungered for his kiss, his touch, every minute of every day. Apparently, that wasn't true for Nick. Had he already forgotten her? Did he not want her anymore?

"I—I came to see Bonnie. Do you mind?" Her voice was shaking as she waited for his response. She was so disappointed that he was staring at her as if he didn't know her at all. Damn it, he'd held her in his arms and made love to her so many times she'd lost count.

He was frowning more ferociously than ever. "No, I don't mind," he growled. "Come on, I'll take you there."

"No, you were catching a plane. I don't want you to miss it. I can manage," she assured him, her heart breaking all over again.

Instead of answering, he grabbed her arm and started toward the exit.

"Nick! I told you I can manage. There's no need to—"

He just pulled her through the door to the pavement and hailed a cab, still saying nothing. Well, fine. She didn't want to talk to him either. Not if this was the welcome he was giving her.

Nick couldn't believe he'd found Liza without ever leaving town. Found her only to hear her say she was coming to visit Bonnie. Hell, he'd been going crazy, not knowing where to find her, yearning to talk with her…to touch her.

If he'd gone with his inclination, he'd have stood her up against a wall and made love to her right there in front of God and everyone. His need for her was so compelling that propriety wasn't important for him. But that need was so much more than sex.

He'd recognized things were different for Liza, as a public figure. And he'd promised himself he'd accept her life as his, doing his best for her, whether it was what he wanted or not. His dream was Liza. Nothing more. So he kept his hands to himself.

She sat next to him in the taxi, her arms folded across her chest, glaring at the back of the driver.

"Did you have a nice flight?" he asked stiffly.

She switched her glare to him. "Fine, thank you."

He ran his tongue over his lips, hoping to still the craving in his gut. The ride to his house had never seemed so long.

"Where were you going?" she asked, staring at the driver again.

He couldn't think of what to say. He wasn't ready to confess how much he needed her. Not in front of the taxi driver. "Uh, I had a consultation."

"For a patient? Tell the driver to turn around. You can still make your flight."

The driver automatically began slowing down to make a U-turn, and Nick ordered him to continue to the address given.

"But, Nick, you're a doctor. You can't —"

"I'll get someone else to cover it." Damn it, all he wanted was to get her to himself, and she kept trying to escape. Had he misjudged everything? Did she not care about him at all?

"I should have called Bonnie," Liza muttered. She was sure Bonnie would welcome her visit, even if Nick didn't. How could she have been so wrong about him? She'd believed he loved her.

Without saying anything, he took out his cell phone and dialed a number. "Bonnie? I'm coming home." After a pause, he said, "She's with me."

Liza watched his face, hoping his involvement with the phone would keep him from seeing her emotions.

"No, never. But I found her in the airport."

Then he handed the phone to Liza. She softly said hello into the receiver and Bonnie screamed.

"I'm sorry I didn't give you more notice that I was coming to visit you," Liza said.

"You know you don't have to give me warning, lovey. You're always welcome here. How far away are you?"

"A few blocks," Liza said. "I'll see you in a minute."

She handed the phone back to Nick with a murmured thank you. "Perhaps you can take a later flight as soon as you drop me off."

He didn't appear grateful for those words. In fact, his face looked sterner than ever, as if he were irritated by her thoughtfulness. Well, too bad. He obviously didn't want her in his house. She'd be sure she left before he came home.

She bit her bottom lip. She'd hoped she was coming home, that she'd never have to leave him. Not only would she have to leave, but she'd have to do so before he came back.

The taxi stopped in front of his lovely home. Before either of them could emerge, Bonnie flung open the front door and came rushing toward them. Grateful that someone was glad to see her, Liza slid from the taxi and held out her arms for Bonnie's welcoming hug.

All the way to the front door, Bonnie petted and exclaimed over her, telling her how glad she was to see her, how she hoped she'd make it a long stay, how much she'd missed her. All the sentiments she'd hoped to hear from Nick.

And he'd said nothing.

She heard him as he entered the house after her, but she ignored him. He could leave now. Then she could cry on Bonnie's shoulder because he didn't want her.

"Come to the kitchen, lovey. I made some cookies for Nick to take with him and there's plenty left over. You have eaten, haven't you?"

Liza shook her head. "I—I decided at the last minute and I didn't have time—" She must've caught the glare on Nick's face. "I truly have been eating. But I was in a hurry—"

"Now, Nick, don't you fuss at our Liza. She came home, didn't she? I'll fix you some soup and a salad. How about that, lovey? It won't take long."

"I'd love it, Bonnie." She smiled at her friend. "I've missed you so much."

Bonnie stopped to hug her again. "I've missed you, lovey," she assured her.

To Liza's surprise, Nick took her arm. "Fix her dinner, Bonnie, but while you're doing so, Liza and I are going to talk."

His grim expression didn't encourage her any. "But you've got to return to the airport to catch your flight," she insisted.

"What—" Bonnie started to say, but Nick stopped her.

"I'll explain later. Just fix the food," he ordered and pulled Liza after him.

She assumed they'd have their discussion in the den, but he headed straight for the stairs. "Why are we going upstairs?"

No answer.

"Do you want me to collect the things I left behind?" she asked. "You want to erase any hint of my stay? I'm sorry if I've inconvenienced you," she added with a definite snit in her voice. Which was his fault. He didn't have to act like all she'd been was a bother.

He pulled her inside his bedroom and slammed the door behind the two of them. Then, much to her surprise, he wrapped his arms tightly around her and kissed her as if he wanted to consume her.

She didn't protest. In fact, for a moment, she forgot all about his bad attitude, since she was so grateful to touch him again. But when he lifted his head, her anger came back.

"Now are you going to catch your plane?"

"No, damn it, I'm not!" He lifted one hand from around her and reached inside his jacket pocket to withdraw his airplane ticket. "Here's the lousy ticket you're so interested in."

She frowned at him, not understanding.

"Take it. Read the destination."

Finally, she did so, still not understanding what he was trying to tell her. Between her heartache and being near him again, she wasn't sure she'd understand anyway.

"Your consultation is in New York City?"

"No," he roared, pulled her tighter against him. "There was no consultation. I was coming to find you."

"You were?" she asked in a whisper, afraid to believe what his words were telling her.

Something in her voice must have encouraged him. "You don't mind, do you?"

With her eyes wide as she devoured the softened expression on his dear face, she said, "No, but you said—"

"Well, damn it! What did you expect me to say? You said you were coming to visit Bonnie, not me!"

"But you were leaving!" she protested.

"To find you!" he repeated.

Realizing they were going in circles, Liza pressed her cheek against his heart, to give her strength, and said, "I wanted to discuss—to talk about the future."

Resting his head against hers, he whispered, "You are my future."

"Oh, Nick!" she exclaimed, tears filling her eyes. "Are you sure? You haven't known me that long, and—"

His lips covered hers again, until she had no breath at all, and no desire to change things as long as he held her in his arms.

When he finally lifted his head once more, he said, "Liza, don't leave me again. I can't survive if you leave me again."

"Oh, Nick, I want to stay forever, but what about...your child?"

"You read those lies?"

"He isn't your little boy?"

"No. Daphne just didn't want me to be happy.

Even if he were, I wouldn't marry Daphne. Only you, sweetheart. I need you."

His kiss this time involved moving closer to the bed, as well as removing articles of clothing so he could touch her skin. Since she addressed his state of dress also, he felt sure he'd interpreted her reaction correctly. And thanked God for it.

Then they fell to the bed in frenzied haste, each acting as a starving person before a buffet, eager to touch and taste every inch of each other. "Oh, Nick, please!" Liza pleaded as she pulled him closer.

He couldn't resist any request from his beloved Liza. He made them one, his hunger driving him beyond belief. When they finally collapsed against each other, he held her in his arms, struggling to regain his breath. The joy of holding her, feeling her against him, believing they would be together only added to his satisfaction.

But he wanted it in words.

"Liza, I love you. Promise you won't ever leave me again."

Her silence wiped out all that satisfaction, all the dizzying happiness. "Liza?"

"Nick, I—I have to tell you some things."

He raised up on one elbow. "Promise me you won't leave," he repeated. She wasn't looking at him, which worried him even more. "Promise!"

"If you want me to stay, I'll stay."

"You know I want you to stay! Why do you sound like you don't want to?"

"I do!" she cried, meeting his gaze. "I do want to

stay. I need to stay," she told him. "I love you, Nick. I'll always love you. But—but I have to tell you something."

"You can have your career, sweetheart. I won't hold you back. I'll do everything I can to help you."

"You want me to sing?" she asked, her voice trembling.

"You have a gift, Liza. I couldn't insist that you walk away from it. It's not my right. If I had my choice, I'd never want you to go anywhere, but you get to make the choices about your career."

To his surprise, she looked relieved. "I thought you might want— A lot of people like the fame that—"

He pulled her against him and kissed her deeply. "I don't care about the fame, sweetheart. I just care about you."

"Oh, Nick, I love you so much."

"I love you, too. Is that it? Have we finished talking? Because I have other things I'd rather be doing, like repeating what we just did. I have a lot of time to make up for."

"No. There's something else."

"What?"

"Do you remember the first night we made love?"

"Oh, yeah."

"I told you I was protected."

"Yeah." He almost stopped breathing. Was she already carrying his child? Was he to be doubly blessed? Liza and a child?

"I said that because I'd been told I probably

couldn't have children. Scar tissue from an earlier operation.''

Nick pulled her close. "I'm sorry, sweetheart. I'm so sorry."

Liza heard the pain in his voice. She struggled to continue.

"They told me when I was eighteen. But—but I'm pregnant, Nick. They were wrong." She held her breath, hoping he'd be happy.

Instead, he merely stared at her. "You're pregnant? With my child?"

"Who else's child would it be?"

Instead of answering, he kissed her. Then the questions burst out of him: "How are you? Have you seen a doctor? Is there anything wrong? We've got a great man here. I'll call in the morning and get an appointment to—"

"Nick! Nick, I've seen a doctor and everything's all right. But—but I don't know if I'll ever be able to have any other children. You have to think about that. You wanted a big family and—and I don't know if—"

He sat straight up in bed and took her by the shoulders to lift her, too. "Is that what this is all about? You're worried I won't want you if you can't provide me with a dozen children? Dear God, Liza. It's you. I want you. I want to live my life with you. If we're blessed with any children, I'll be thrilled. But you're the one I can't live without."

And he kissed her again.

"Oh, Nick, I wanted you to say that. But are you sure? I'd understand if—"

"Well, I wouldn't! We're getting married as soon as we can get a license."

"I'll want to tell Emily. I know she can't come, but I want to tell her."

"Of course. And my family, my brothers and sister. And your parents?"

Liza snuggled against him, finding it hard to believe she was discussing her wedding. "Hmm, let's wait until after we're married. I want to enjoy my wedding."

He grinned. "Agreed. I certainly want to enjoy our wedding. And the rest of our lives. Us and junior here," he added softly, touching her stomach.

"You won't mind if the baby's a girl?"

"Of course not, as long as you don't mind if I teach her to fish," he teased.

A knock sounded on the door. Liza pulled the sheet up to her chin. Nick made sure he was covered too. "Yes?"

"Nick, I have Liza's soup ready."

"Did you bring it up?"

"Yes."

"Then come on in." He knew how anxious Bonnie was to find out what was going on.

When she discovered them both in bed together, Bonnie grinned. "I guess I don't have to ask if she's going to stay?"

Nick grinned in return. "She's more than just staying. We're getting married."

"Hallelujah!" Bonnie set the tray on a table by the door and rushed to hug them both.

"Bonnie?" Nick said after he'd received his hug. "There's one more thing."

"What's that?" she asked, her face covered with a beaming smile.

Knowing how much his housekeeper would celebrate with them, like the mother she pretended to be, he said softly, "We're having a baby."

Bonnie screamed with joy as she started the hugging all over again. "Oh, lovey, I prayed and prayed. This is wonderful. I'm going to be a grandma!" Then she backed away from the bed. "I mean, um, I'll be a stand-in grandma."

Liza grinned. "I think you'll be the best grandma ever, Bonnie. I'll need your help. I don't know much about being pregnant or having a baby."

"Oh, lovey, I'd be so proud to help you. Now, the first thing is you need to eat your dinner and get your rest. Nick, don't you be bothering her. Let her sleep," she ordered sternly, backing toward the door. "I've got fresh milk for in the morning, lovey. We're going to take good care of our baby." She beamed at both of them and left the room.

"Uh-oh, I think we're going to regret telling her so soon," Nick said. "She's going to hover over you like crazy."

"No, I won't regret it," she assured him. "I'm going to love every minute. It'll be like having Aunt Meredith back. Like having a family." She kissed him. "There's just one problem."

"What's that?" Nick asked anxiously.

"I'm not the least bit sleepy. Can you help me with that?"

"Are you sure? What about dinner?"

"Nick, I've been gone too long. I'll eat later. Bonnie will never know."

He pulled her close, reveling in her soft skin. "Oh, yeah, I think I can help."

Both their dreams were coming true.

The Colton family saga continues with
FROM BOSS TO BRIDEGROOM
by Victoria Pade in October 2001.
Don't miss it!

One

Rand Colton was on Lucy's mind. He'd been there when she'd gone to bed Friday night, he'd been there the moment she woke up Saturday morning, he'd been there all weekend and he was still there Monday morning even before her alarm went off, as she lay in bed.

It was very troubling.

Not only couldn't she stop thinking about him, but her thoughts…

Very troubling, indeed.

She'd had no business thinking about him kissing her. *Vividly* thinking about him kissing her. No business at all. She had to be out of her mind.

He was her boss. He was a workaholic over-achiever who didn't even want a single mother for him, let alone in any more personal role. And she had better not lose sight of it because he was a fascinating man.

And he was that, she had to admit.

A fascinating man who also happened to be great-looking, more man than she'd ever met and a brilliant attorney—the kind she'd wanted to be herself before fate had stepped in and made that impossible.

Rand Colton was a fascinating man who also happened to be charming and suave and sophisticated, with a good sense of humor and an admirable strength in his convictions.

What are you, his biggest fan? she asked herself.

Maybe he should have hired her to do his public relations work instead of his secretarial work.

Oh, yeah, her thoughts were troubling, all right.

She'd just met him and here she was ticking off enough attributes to make him sound like Superman.

It just wouldn't do.

But then none of the places her thoughts were leading her would do.

She had enough on her plate taking care of Max and trying to support them both, she reminded herself. She didn't have time for daydreams like she'd fallen into all weekend. Let alone time for a relationship or a romance—even if a relationship or a romance was what Rand Colton was offering.

And it wasn't.

So why was she having such a hard time getting him off her mind when she knew better?

Maybe it was a result of deprivation. There was no

denying that she was a young, vital woman who hadn't had a date in almost five years. And not only that, she also spent most of her time in the company of a four-year-old. It wasn't even unusual for her to go days without so much as speaking to another adult, especially since quitting her job at the Bar Association library a month ago to make this move to Washington.

So she could make an argument for having been deprived of contact with people her own age, along with being deprived of contact with a man.

Given that, it only made sense that a few hours out in the adult world with someone like Rand Colton would go to her head.

But that was all there was to it, she tried to convince herself. A rebound effect of social and interpersonal deprivation.

And when the man she was out in the adult world with was a man like Rand Colton—a man impossible for any woman not to find attractive—of course she was attracted. Of course her mind was doing some natural wandering. Some natural wondering. Some fantasizing.

But fantasizing was harmless enough, she reasoned. As long as she didn't act on any of it.

And as long as he didn't know what was going on. Or did he?

She hoped not. But she *had* escaped her own kissing ruminations to find him smiling that smile at her, as if he'd been able to read her every thought like closed-captioning at the bottom of a television screen.

No, that was just silly. He could have had any number of things on his mind to cause that smile.

Still, he'd been looking at her, studying her, which meant the smile might have been an indication that he liked what he saw.

Now *that* was a dangerous possibility, Lucy realized, annoyed with her once-again-wandering thoughts.

Worse than being attracted to him was the idea that he might have been attracted to her.

She didn't need that.

Oh sure, it would be a nice boost to her ego. But look what the last boost to her ego had gotten her— Max and raising him alone.

Only this time she wouldn't be able to say she hadn't been warned about what the man was all about. Rand Colton had made himself perfectly clear. No kids. Period.

"So stop thinking about him," she whispered to herself in the predawn darkness of her bedroom as if the spoken word would have more impact.

She really had to stop thinking about how much she'd enjoyed working with him—despite how demanding he was and how high were his expectations.

She had to stop thinking about how much she'd enjoyed bantering with him, debating the child issue, having dinner with him.

She had to stop thinking about cobalt blue eyes and mile-wide shoulders, and thighs that tested the limits of his impeccably tailored trousers, and hands that could cup the entire back of her head against the pressure of a kiss...

"Stop it, stop it, stop it!" she said more forcefully. She honestly did not want to be thinking the things she was thinking. She honestly didn't want to be attracted to any man. And she honestly didn't want any boosts to her ego that could make her vulnerable again.

Yes, Max had come out of that vulnerability and she adored her son. No, she wouldn't change anything that would mean he wasn't in her life.

But she couldn't afford to risk anything that might make history repeat itself, either. She couldn't afford it financially or emotionally.

Max's father had hurt her terribly. He hurt her all over again every time Max asked why he didn't have a dad like other kids did.

Lucy would never willingly open herself or Max to more of the grief that had already been caused by a man whose life was clearly set on one course. A man who had no interest, no inclination, no intention whatsoever of altering that course to accommodate a woman with a child.

"So get your head out of the clouds, Lucy," she told herself as her alarm went off.

Because getting involved with a man like Rand Colton once was enough. In fact it was absolutely, unequivocally more than enough.

Where love comes alive™

From first love to forever, these love stories are for today's woman with traditional values.

A highly passionate, emotionally powerful and always provocative read.

♥ *Silhouette*®

SPECIAL EDITION™

Emotional, compelling stories that capture the intensity of living, loving and creating a family in today's world.

♥ *Silhouette*®

INTIMATE MOMENTS™

A roller-coaster read that delivers romantic thrills in a world of suspense, adventure and more.

Visit Silhouette at www.eHarlequin.com

SDIR2